Dope Boi Diaries

Jeremy Jae Jae Davis

Merie Vision Publishing
Merievisionpublishing@gmail.com

ISBN: 978-1-961213-11-1
Library of Congress control number on record

Formatting, Editing, and Design by
Merie Vision Publishing, LLC

First Print Edition: May 2024

Printed in the United States of America

Acknowledgments

I would like to take this opportunity to think my amazing support system at Lawrenceville Correctional Center. My OG, Richard Gun, out of Danville. He is sixty-four and has read every Uptown Classic I've ever written no cap. Rodney Brown aka. Dre, you a lock for the movie phew. I tell him the entire book before it's published and he still reads it, that's love.

Big Will, my security, thanks lil-big bro. Dewayne Hill aka Sheikh, my Muslim brother. My Uptown Mobb, Coolie, Park Terrence, Joe, Norview Buck, RG, Fortworth Bump Beezy. Mark Kelly aka Sabir, my St. Louis brother. Cori Thomas aka TMac. Mark Manley. aka Lil-Man, you know I got you Ace another one of my day one supporters. Big Ruck who always calling me Tyler Perry. I take that as a compliment all day, Ace! Swing, aka Larry, out of Danville, it's the same positive vibe with bro. What's Poppin Buzzo! The homie out of DMV, Tyrone Smith aka Freaky, he gave me a couple of ideas and we came up with my best seller Masked. Steven Pannell, aka SP, he capped my first book Kandy when I first presented it to him, but after he realized I was official with the pen, he hasn't missed one book. I appreciate the love, Ace.

I promise I wont stop giving you all my best creativity. It's only the beginning. Your love and support is greatly appreciated. I'ma definitely see a few of you on the red carpet beside me. Be on the lookout for more exclusive content on the way.

This has been another Uptown Classic and Merie Visions Publication. We taking over the industry one book at a time.

<u>One</u>

I was born on September 3rd to a single mother of three boys and two girls. With me being the youngest of the five, I was born a premature asthmatic baby, due to my mother's addiction to cigarettes and marijuana during her seven-month pregnancy. Fortunately, I overcame the battle and fought my way into the world. I'm grateful to be able to say, I grew up a healthy, happy, and spoiled child.

I can vividly recall growing up in the projects called Lafayette Shores. It was located in the heart of Norfolk VA, just off of the 664 Tidewater Drive exit. Everyone who resided there were like family. The minute you entered the neighborhood it felt like home. Our neighborhood was overly littered with broken bottles and trash. To an outsider, it looked polluted and impoverished, but somehow, we turned a blind eye to it. Seeing trash and broken glass was the norm.

Lafayette Shores was enormously big. They say it was one of the biggest housing developments back in the eighties. Some units were two-story, but majority of them were one-story bungalows lined up side by side. Because of how close the houses were, everyone looked

out for one another and their children. Get caught
doing something you weren't supposed to be doing and
Miss Loretta, Miss Brenda, Miss Michelle, and even
Miss Gwen from up the street, would whip your "hind
parts." Then, would take you inside of their houses to
clean you up and feed you. Your mother wouldn't
even have a problem with it…those were the days.

The love and the energy was genuine and the
money was plentiful. Whatever your hustle, no matter
what it was, you were likely to succeed at it. As I reflect
on my life, I can honestly say that Lafayette Shores was
the foundation and the essence of how I came about
being who I am and how the birth of the hustler in me,
was originated.

My mother was a certified hustler. Seven days a
week, three hundred and sixty-five days a year, she got
to the bag. I admired her. At the age of twenty-five,
she worked at the local motel called The Scottish Inn,
just off of military highway during the day. After she
completed her eight-hour shift, she would come home
and begin her second hustle, which was hosting socials
and games throughout the evening. Her dinners would
consist of fried fish, or chicken dinners, with a side of
french fries, along with a refreshment of her famous
sun-made iced tea that she made inside of a pickle jar
and would allow the sun to "cook" throughout the
evening. That was and is still the best damn tea, I've

ever drank. She also had Icehouse beer and liquor shots, which were two dollars a pop.

All day, everyday, our house reeked the smell of marijuana and chicken grease while Bob Marley and the Wailers, "No Woman, No Cry," Cameo, "Just Like Candy," and Bobby Brown's, "Don't Be Cruel," consistently played in the background.

My mother would even host game nights of Tonk, Spades, and Poker games. Each game was set up in different bedrooms. Every child in the house had their fair share of the profits. My oldest sister, Christine, served all the drinks to the guests. As long as they were buying food and gambling, their drinks were free. My Uncle Chris ran back and forth to the corner and liquor stores for my mother. My brother, Terry, would spin the records, while Marcus, my other brother, would watch over the festivities making sure everything went smoothly.

At the end of the night, we all helped to clean up and put the furniture back in its place. Everyone had a part to play. Afterward, my mother would sit down, count out money, and begin paying each child their gap. I guess you could say it was our family hustle.

My mother also sold marijuana out of potato sack baggies. Back in the early eighties, they called good marijuana reefer or sess. On the weekends, she would allow the local hustlers she knew, or once dated, shoot craps in my bedroom.

At that time, I couldn't have been any more than five years old, but I can recall plenty of nights observing, from the top of my bunk bed, crowds of big people excited to be throwing shiny white rocks on the floor. I curiously found myself wondering just what they were doing and why, before every roll, did they ask me to blow over their shiny rocks. I have to admit, I kind of enjoyed blowing on their shiny rocks because, for some reason, they would get excited after each roll. When all of the festivities were finally over and the big people left my room, I could easily count out a handful of those green pieces of paper. At five years old and in the early eighties, that was a grip. My mother lived by one rule…you have to pay to play.

Since my bedroom was the biggest in our house, my mother allowed the hustlers to shoot craps there as long as they were giving me my fifty-cent cut after every three dice rollers. I don't know if it was because they respected my mother's house rules, or if it was because my older brother, Marcus, would peep his head into my bedroom to check the temperature while holding his signature mini-Louisville slugger baseball bat every so often. I can say I never witnessed an argument or fight, and I always got my money. It was later revealed to me that my brother Marcus was one of the most feared killers in the city, and for that reason alone, I admired him.

We moved to Uptown and I began to witness a transformation in myself. I can recall being distant and not wanting to play or socialize with my peers. I was used to being around my older sister and brothers all day, so I didn't want to play outside. Then, things changed and my mother no longer hosted her nightly socials. Being used to the money, both my brothers took their hustle to the streets. I would always want to follow behind them and every time, for the good in me, they would tell me to go and play somewhere.

I looked up and admired them because, in my opinion, they were the flyest guys I'd ever known. Not to mention, they had all the girls, money, and cars. My brother Terry turned into a scammer. He linked up with some wealthy African man from Ghana and began selling information on the Dark Web. He would soon become rich from stealing the identities of military soldiers. For fifteen hundred dollars, you could get their entire identity, if they were alive and for three thousand, if they were deceased.

My brother Marcus was the knee baby. He sold drugs and offered murder-for-hire services. He didn't care who it was, if the price was right, he was coming for your head. I remembered him being loved by a few, but feared by many. He was a cold-hearted mothafucka and I believe that to this day. I developed a portion of both of their personalities and traits, but a much bigger portion of my personality and my looks came from Marcus. I can recall people telling me, all the time, how identical we were.

Marcus was later killed at the corner of Church Street and Virginia, Beach Blvd. He was ambushed at a red light. The coroner's report stated that he was shot over sixty-four times in his chest and head. Dead at the age of nineteen with a closed casket at his funeral. That day will live in me forever. That day changed me, and the way I looked at life…

All the boys my age wanted to play Contra, Street Fighter, Super Mario Brothers, Techmo Bowl, watch wrestling, and do flips on pissy-ass mattresses. From growing up around my brothers, I knew that wasn't going to get me any fly gear, money, or girls. Most of the time, my friends just ended up with ringworms on their necks or in their heads. I was too fly for all that. I guess you can say I was ahead of my time.

Back then, especially in Uptown, you had official dope boys. You know, the ones you could actually count on one hand. We were also trendsetters, had our own style, and our own lingo. Nobody, and I mean nobody, could say Nephew, Family, Cool, or Ace like an Uptown nigga! Trust me, we could always tell the difference.

We also had hood Legends like Fat Bobby, Ricky Williams, Stacy Rodgers, and Ant Collins. These were the hustlers I knew and looked up to. Uptown was just different. It was the home to fashion. We sported the latest gear from Used, Kansas, Tommy Hilfiger, Nautica, and Guess Jeans. Along with the Butter Softs, Shearling, 8 ball leathers, Triple Fat Goose, Avirex, and NFL starter jackets. We would often sport gold fronts in our mouths, along with a Cuban link or herringbone gold chain around our necks. We would top it off, with a fresh Nautica, Tommy, or Polo shirt. Our shoe game, hands down, had to be official. That was law. We would often sport a crisp pair of DC Nikes, wheat Timberland's, the field Beef and Broccoli's, Polo, and Gortex boots. I can't forget to mention the original Nike Air Jordans. Our dress code and Uptown swag was incomparable. We actually grew up some fly young niggas.

School was fun, but learning was the last thing on my mind. All I cared about was gear, basketball, and girls. I remember my first crush, Janice Jones. She was a fly Uptown shorty. She was cute as hell, and she had a big ole booty. I used to palm it every chance I got, without her permission. She would always look at me and just shake her head. Now that I look back at it, I was a perverted individual. Janice had me mesmerized by her voluptuous body and pretty face. I knew she liked me, because she had four older brothers, and not once had she threatened to tell on me. I still remember the first time I approached her after school. I was in the seventh grade attending Ruffner Middle.

"Ayeee, Janice!!

"What boy?" she replied while strutting up the street, walking like somebody's grown-ass mother. I loved a confident walk and she had it.

"I know you heard me calling you," I replied walking towards her trying to catch my breath. She stood with her left hand on her hips as if she had some place to be and I was holding her up or something. "What you doing this weekend?" I asked.

The newly built, Macarthur Mall, was in walking distance and just up the block from our neighborhood. All of the local kids hung out there on the weekends, and it was said to be the newest hot spot. I offered to take her there on a lunch date. A couple of weeks went by and, eventually, Janice took me up on my offer. We sat talked and ate lunch at the Cheesecake factory. After, I decided to catch a cab to the Cinemark

Cinemas across town at the Military Circle Mall to watch the latest blockbuster movie, Love and Basketball. I knew it was more ghetto and acceptable there seeing teenagers make out in the back.

Janice wanted popcorn, Milk Duds, and Mike and Ikes. I wasn't tripping. She could of gotten the whole concession stand because all my little horny ass wanted to do was get my feel on. I had no intention of watching the movie. The popcorn was still hot, the previews and credits were rolling, and I'd already begun caressing her thick thighs and tongue-kissing her neck. That was the best feeling ever.

After she watched the movie, we stood outside and waited for our cab to arrive. I stood behind her continuing to kiss her neck and rub on her booty, while telling her all the things I wanted to do to her. Suddenly, she cut me off, turned around, and asked if I would like to stay the night at her house.

Now at this time, I was unaware of two things. One, that she wasn't a virgin. Second, unbeknownst to me, she was dating a senior football all-American at the time. We arrived at her apartment and she invited me in.

"Come in? I repeated what she just said to me back to her as if I hadn't heard her the first time.

"Yes, and be quiet. My mother's drunk again, sleeping on the couch," she replied.

We entered her bedroom, and she began to strip ass naked, instantly. I couldn't believe what was happening right before my virgin eyes. I stood in shock. See, back then, a set of boobs would drive me insane, and Janice had the sexiest A-cups, I'd ever seen.

"Take your clothes off," she said.

I stood nervous as hell, shaking like a stripper. Janice noticed and began laughing. "I know Mr. Nasty is not the big V," she said with this devious smirk on her face.

"Not really," I lied, "it's just been a while," I said embarrassed, still standing in my Timberlands, t-shirt, and boxers.

"Oh, so you just like to talk freaky, and grind all over me, getting my panties all sticky and wet, huh? That's not fair, Brian," she said, moving closer to me.

Suddenly, she pulled my boxers down and told me to lay back, relax, and breathe. She could tell I was nervous. I laid back on her bed and covered my entire face with both my hands, while she took me to a place I never even knew existed.

I climaxed within a matter of minutes. It frightened the life out of me, but at the same time, it felt amazing! It almost felt like the first time I experienced smoking high-grade marijuana, but ten times the pleasure. After that night, I was on a mission to experience that feeling over, again, and, again for the rest of my life.

That was the day I became a man and, unfortunately, the last time I would ever see Janice Jones again. She died in a car accident Thanksgiving Day on her way home returning from shopping at the local Rack' n Sack grocery store. The coroner's toxicology report stated that her mother, Juanita Jones, blood alcohol level was 0.19 percent. Drunk was an understatement. From that day forward, I made a promise to myself, that I would never drink alcohol. Seeing somebody one day and they're gone the next can really fuck with your mental.

My second crush was Nikki. She was quiet and cute as a button. She never spoke much, but her body language spoke volumes. Standing at 5"3, 140 pounds of thickness, physically, she was everything I wanted in a girlfriend, but back then, I thought I was God's gift to women. For some strange reason, I expected Nikki to approach me.

It's crazy because we both knew and felt the physical attraction, but neither one of us had the confidence to break the ice. I experienced that feeling almost every day during the entire school year. I finally had the opportunity to speak my peace. I was now a more confident and mature young man. It happened my senior year. Nikki had transferred from Bayside back to Booker T. Washington High. I was seventeen, driving a sky-blue Nissan box Maxima sitting on eighteen-inch rims. I bumped into her at the local Norfolk State 7-Eleven. I remember it like it was yesterday. I was sitting in my car, drinking my favorite Welches grape soda, eating barbecue sunflower seeds, rolling a Philly blunt, and listening to The Notorious B.I.G. when suddenly, I noticed a female walking past my vehicle.

I only caught a glimpse of her entering the store from the back, but that was enough to get my attention because her walk looked instinctively familiar. I exited my vehicle, entered the store, and immediately recognized her. How could I ever forget my second crush?

"I see you still got that mean ass walk, Nakia Suarez."

"I see you grew a mustache, Brian Bishop."

We both began laughing. "It's so good to see you again!" I said, undressing her with my eyes.

Nikki was a sexy-ass redbone, with light green eyes. She also had an attractive smile. I couldn't keep my eyes off of her and she smelled amazing. I've always found it attractive when a woman smells good.

I eventually told her how much I crushed on her throughout our elementary and junior high school years. She laughed and said she couldn't believe that I never approached her. She eventually admitted that she had a crush on me as well. She said that she was a cosmetologist and she worked part-time at the beauty salon just a couple doors down from the 7-Eleven. She asked me to stop by sometime whenever I was in the neighborhood. I agreed that I would and we exchanged numbers before I exited the store.

I sat in my Nissan Maxima blasting, "One Mo' Chance," through my Fosgate audio speakers. Then, Nikki exited the store and I couldn't take my eyes off her. It was something about her walk and confidence that won me over. I believe she knew her worth and she knew she was a baddie.

Nikki ended up calling me later that day just to ask me twenty-one hundred questions like, "What have I been doing? Why was I single? Whose vehicle was I driving?"

I was surprised by her questions. It was almost as if she thought you weren't supposed to be driving at seventeen. I just don't like walking…that was my reasoning, but the attention I began receiving from my peers was intoxicating. At Booker T. Washington High, I was amongst the elite of dope boys, hustlers, and trendsetters. Honestly, having a car came with that status.

I fell deeply in love with fashion. I loved getting fresh every day, and the best part of it all was, I could actually afford to dress myself. That was and had always been the plan because Booker T. Washington High was known as the fashion capital of high schools. If you weren't fresh from head to toe, you might as well stay home. I knew a lot of kids who sold drugs only to buy clothes because they attended that school. So, you can only imagine the dropout rate.\

My brother, Terry, had been incarcerated for a year and I was on a mission to get him a lawyer. So, I hustled weed and crack cocaine from sun up to sun down in Uptown between Wide Street and Smith and Bagnall. I can recall coming in my mother's house around six in the morning with my pockets stuffed with cash. I couldn't even imagine seeing my mother downstairs that early, but on this particular morning, she so happened to be up and awake the minute I entered through the front door. The aroma of Folger's coffee and Newports filled the living room. My mother was sitting in her favorite spot on her couch watching Wavy News Ten.

She looked up, with her evil look, and asked, "What the hell you doing coming in my house at six in the damn morning!?"

I remember bluntly saying that I've been hustling. At that very moment, I couldn't believe that I had just said that. My mother wasn't even surprised. As a matter of fact, she knew the entire time. Mothers are blessed with that intuition, and they know their children. Plus, it had been almost a full year since she had brought me anything.

"Okay hustler!" she replied, blowing a thick wad of cigarette smoke in my direction. "It's time to start paying some bills around here. Let's start with the rent!" she said, holding her hand out.

"How much?" I asked.

"Five hundred," she replied.

I knew my mother's rent wasn't that much because we stayed in the projects. I turned my back and began counting out five hundred dollars in tens, twenties, and fifties. I turned back around and handed it over to her.

"I'ma need two hundred for food, and another hundred on the water and cable bill."

I left and went upstairs to my shoe box stash and counted out an extra fifty. I returned and passed her three more hundred. She shook her head and immediately passed it back.

"You think you a man now, huh? You think you have life all figured out right?" I stood silent while she talked. "Brian, that life you living is not going to last. You didn't learn shit from your brothers, huh? Your lil' black ass is going to be in jail no sooner than later. Don't be expecting no money or visits from me, and if you had any sense, you would start putting some of that money away for a good lawyer because you're going to need one!"

See, my mother was a Certified Gee. She had been around pimps, killers, and hustlers her entire life, so there was no tricking her. She could smell a dope dealer from a mile away. She was never okay with the fact that I was selling drugs. She just wanted to make sure I could take care of myself. She never wanted the money. The money was the test, but I had already been bitten by the drug bug. I loved having money! It made me happy…nothing else mattered to me.

TWO

Nikki started attending nursing school during the day and was doing hair appointments at night. Our schedules didn't coincide, so we barely seen each other. The Roman poet, Sextus, said, "Time and distance make the heart grow fonder." I was hoping this was true because we were young and just starting life, but I knew Nikki was the one for me.

By this time, I was already knee-deep into the streets. I moved out of my mother's house and began saving my money. Even when I began shopping, my mother's voice would always be in the back of my mind telling me to save for a lawyer. Life was good, but it could have been better. I needed my own independence, my own house, and my own responsibilities. My box Maxima was butter, but that new 300E Mercedes Benz was screaming my name!

I ran into an old friend of mine named Black from Uptown. Our mothers were best friends, so I distinctly remember plenty of nights when we slept in the same bed while playing Contra, Tecmo Bowl, Tetris Mario Brothers, and R.B.I. baseball. Decades had passed, and even though our parents were still friends, me and Black hadn't seen or talked to one another until I ran into him at the local convenience store. I had heard many stories about him over the years being the plug, but I never got around to getting his number from his mother whenever she would show up to visit my mother.

"What's good Black?"

"It's been a while! "

"How is Miss Gwen doing?" I asked.

"She's doing fine. How is your mother, sister, and brother doing?"

"Everybody's hanging in there," I replied. "I'm still trying to stack this bread up, so I can get Terry a good defense attorney."

"Yeah, I heard through a friend of mine that he was one of the people who got caught up in that stimulus and IPP loan fraud scheme. He lucky that didn't go federal. Here, take my number and hit me around five-thirty. I have a trap house on C Avenue." Black wrote his number and address down on his receipt paper.

I arrived at his trap house about an hour later. Immediately, I noticed he was running shit. Black's presence was big and not everyone was kissing his ass. He had, at least, five females sitting around. He also had two guys watching the front and back doors holding guns. The other three were in the kitchen cooking coke. A few of the women were bagging and tagging the product. Others were serving the crack fiends through a man-made hole in the back door.

Guns, weed, and crack were everywhere. I began to notice that everyone in the spot feared Black, but the Black I've always known was humble and laid back. I would soon discover that Black had a dark side to him. It didn't take long for me to notice his alcohol and drug problem. I'd observed him on many occasions snorting dope and drinking to the point of unconsciousness.

His trap house averaged around fifteen to twenty grand a day. All of his workers were paid at the end of each week. Since I had a vehicle and a hustler's ambition, he recruited me, and I became his top lieutenant. He sold me crack for a low price and would allow me to sell my product out of his trap house, but only after all of his product had been sold out. That was cool with me, because the trap rolled so hard, that we could never keep enough product anyways. Everything we touched sold out that day or by the end of the night. Black's trap spot was run and operated like a well-oiled machine.

After a successful month run working for Black, I managed to stack me a cool twenty- five grand.

Everything was going good and I had no complaints. Except, one Friday evening I walked into the trap, and I heard Black yelling at the top of his lungs while shooting his gun into the floor. He scared the living hell out of two workers and told them to strip ass naked in front of everyone in the spot.

"What the hell?" I responded, looking confused.

"Bishop! My nigga!" he said the minute he noticed me. "These poe ass pieces of shit been stealing from us," he yelled.

I could tell he was high and drunk. His eyes were bloodshot red, and his fresh white polo shirt was drenched in sweat.

"Bishop, what should I do?"

He always called me by my last name, so I stayed with it. I still remember the look on both of the kid's faces.

"Just let them go, bro! They've been brought. We have been nothing but good to them. It's their lost. They won't get money like this anywhere else," I said, hoping he would listen.

"Mannn!! I wanna kill these muthafucka's!" he yelled, before shooting into the house floor again.

"My Gee, we getting too much money. The last thing we need is the police shutting down our operation and stopping this cash flow behind a couple of dollars. We too rich for that shit," I said.

At that moment I observed what looked to be a calming to the storm kicking in. Black took a deep breath and said to the two thieves, "Tell him thank you because he just saved both of your lives."

They both said thank you to me at the same time while getting dressed, but Black couldn't just leave it there. After he smoked his blunt, he proceeded to walk towards the two thieves and he gun butted them both with his chrome forty-five on the top of their heads. Both of them were bleeding profusely. He told them to never show their faces again before he stormed out of the front door.

Disgusted, I stood there for a second, looking at these cowards calling themselves men. I asked the girls to clean up the blood and then I told the thieves to get the hell out! They didn't hesitate to exit through the door. I could of took that moment and parted ways, but I was, in no way, intimidated by Black. As a matter of fact, I took a liking to him because he reminded me so much of my brother Marcus, in a way. The only difference was that Marcus would have killed the two thieves and everyone else in the house.

Nikki, from the outside, you would have thought was spoiled. She dressed her ass off and kept her nails, feet, and hair done. She lived out Lake Edwards, a predominantly black community bordering Norfolk and Virginia Beach. For our second date, she asked me to pick her up from the local 7-Eleven, again. I waited in my new Lexus as she bent the corner looking amazing.

"You okay?" I asked.

"Yes, why?" she replied.

"I was just asking!"

It wasn't every day that you would pick up your date at a 7-Eleven, but I didn't want her to think I was all up in her business because I was doing me also. I just reminded myself that I was going to ask her about this pickup spot.

We went to Military Circle Mall and like always, I made sure she was good. She never wanted much though. She was more into six-inch stilettos, leather jackets, and miniskirts -the type of clothes I love seeing my women in.

After we left the mall, we stopped and grabbed a bite to eat at the China Garden Buffet. I mostly ate shrimp fried rice and egg rolls. Nikki ate General Tso chicken and egg rolls. Our date night went pleasantly well. On the drive back to Lake Edwards, just as expected, she asked to be dropped off at the 7-Eleven.

"It's eleven o'clock at night," I said. "Nikki, I can't do that." I had been waiting for this moment all night. "No real man would ever agree to something like this. I don't care about whatever situation you have going on, I just want to make sure you're home and safe, baby."

Surprisingly, she agreed and allowed me to take her home. I figured it would all come to a head tonight whatever it was. I had my gun, so I wasn't tripping. She lived in the middle of two adjacent apartments, which I could clearly see the lights on. The house in the middle was completely dark.

"Is anyone home?" I asked.

"No," she replied.

Looking towards her apartment, I observed what looked to be a kid peeping out the window.

"What's going on Nikki? Talk to me. I would hate to assume," I said, turning my car off and looking her directly in her eyes.

She went on to say that she had been living with her crack-addicted auntie and her four badass children. They just recently fell on hard times financially and their lights were temporarily cut off. She said she had made plans on taking the heels and leather jacket I'd purchased for her back to the store to get the money to pay the light bill.

"Damn," I said, "I've experienced hard times, but never like that."

I told her to be up early in the morning and I would be through so that we could go and handle whatever she needed done. I could see the joy all over her face the minute I said that. Suddenly, to my surprise, she leaned over and kissed me with her sweet, soft, and moist lips. I crumbled like a cookie.

Black and I met up in a black alley behind the Food Lion on College Street. He had two people in the trunk that he said owed him money, but knowing him, I figured he was lying. He cocked the gun back, handed it to me, and walked away.

Black had relocated the trap house from C-Avenue to 41st near the campus of Old Dominion University, another known spot to sell pills, coke, and marijuana. We didn't waste a single second. The minute we received the key to the apartment, we began pumping our product out of the front and back doors to all the locals and college kids.

Then, Black began making sudden out-of-town runs. He would tell me to hold the fort down while he was traveling and networking, but word had gotten back to me. I was told that he was actually going out of town doing hits and killing the suppliers. I acted as if I hadn't heard as much, knowing good and well I'd been on missions with him myself.

The first time I saw a duffle bag full of bricks of cocaine, was the day Black entered the trap house and dumped the contents in the bag on the table.

"Damn, that's a lot of coke, my nigga!" I said, observing the white powdery substance.

"Each one of these are 1008 grams, "he said excitedly. "I'm going to teach you how to cook so we can get rich quick, my nigga! Straight breakdown. No weight, No nothing."

Black called Tracy, Unique, Kim, and Meka into the kitchen. Their job was to bag and tag the product. They knew Black was a nut case, so stealing wasn't even an option in their minds. When I arrived, it was only five women workers. Later, I found out it was actually six women all altogether. There was a missing girl named Ebony. Word on the street was she came up missing a couple of weeks after she had stolen money from Black.

Eventually, her remains were found floating in the Elizabeth River with a cinder block attached to both legs. It was also said that she died from two shots to the head. That's when I began to realize this nigga Black was a dangerous lunatic!

I couldn't believe I allowed Black to talk me into being on his fucking payroll. He began paying me four grand a week just to look over his operation whenever he wasn't available. My responsibility was to make sure all the drugs and money were accounted for after each package was sold, but I would never get caught alive sitting in one of our trap houses. They either called or would meet me around the corner. At times, I would just pop up real quick to collect the money and whatever drugs we had left from the package and leave. Good day, or bad day, Black always wanted to know the count.

Nikki emerged from her house busting through her grey Nautica sweatsuit. She couldn't hide all that booty if she wanted to! She sported a pair of grey suede 574 New Balance sneakers with her hair in a wrap. This was my first time seeing her dressed down ever.

"Good morning!" she greeted me with the biggest smile.

"Good morning, beautiful. You looking right cute and thick this morning. I know I have to marry you."

She responded with the most beautiful smile I'd ever seen.

"Where too?" I asked.

She replied, "To pay the bills, right?" as if she didn't know the count.

"Of course," I replied.

We drove to the farm fresh on Providence Rd to pay the light bill. It totaled up to six hundred and fifty dollars with the late fee added. Nikki felt bad and I could tell. She kept saying she really didn't think it was going to be that much! I assured her that it was something light. After I paid the electric bill, I passed her another five hundred for food since we were already in the grocery store. With no electricity, I knew they didn't have any food. I just wanted to see her happy. No person or child should be in the dark or without hot running water or food. That's why I enjoyed hustling sometimes because I could help others in their time of need without hurting my pockets.

Ms. Karen, her aunt, bumped into me a couple of weeks later at the gas station and thanked me. She said that if the rent office had found out that her lights were off, she would have been evicted. I was just glad I was able to help.

For his own personal reasons, Black trusted me when it came to money and drugs. One, because I didn't do drugs, and two, because I'd already had money before we even connected. It seemed as if I was always being tested for weakness by him, but like I said, my lifestyle and energy was aligned with the universe. So, he had no choice but to love me.

One Saturday night, Black decided he was going to take a trip out of town out of the blue. That night, we were all celebrating Meka's birthday at the Red Roof Inn when he made the announcement. He called me into the bathroom, gave me the rundown, and told me to hold down the fort.

"You already know!" I replied, dapping him up before he exited the bathroom.

He left me with five older females that were all drunk and drugged the fuck up. I can't even count the times I said no thank you to the lines of coke and dope they offered me throughout the night. They even got naked and began having sex with one another. I watched as Unique sprinkled lines of coke on Tracy's big ass. Once again, offering me a taste. Just like the last twenty times they asked, I respectfully declined.

"Come on Bishop," Meka cried. "I want some man meat!"

Now that, I was willing to help provide. Without further ado, I walked over, pulled my Johnson out, and allowed the birthday girl to eat up. See, as long as Meka had known me, I was drug-free. So, I didn't understand why she was so adamant on getting me to snort lines of coke and dope. Then, it came to me and a light bulb went on in my head…this nigga Black! It was one of his many tests. *He tried it, but with Unique and Meka's bird brain asses though?* That thought had me laughing to myself. Black had to come better than that.

For my own personal reasons, I would never have sex with Tracy or Unique. My first reason was that they indulged in too many illicit drug activities. Second, I'd walked in on them having sex with different tricks. I hated to see decent-looking females throw their life away. The furthest I ever took it with Unique was allowing her to give me some head. She did it ass naked too! It took everything in me not to bend her pretty ass over. It was tempting, but I stood strong and maintained.

I was Uptown eating at Aunt Dorian's when I received a call from Nikki. I had just finished smoking a half blunt of Kush and was eating my dinner. I ordered two plates, one to eat and another for takeout. It was fried honey barbecue chicken wings with a sauce so sweet and tangy you could eat it by itself. Collard greens without the pork, sweet, candied yams with marshmallows, mouth-watering baked mac and cheese, and buttermilk homemade biscuits…heaven on earth.

"Hello…" I answered my phone on the fourth ring.

"Hello Bishop, were you busy or something?" Nikki asked.

"No, why you ask that?"

"Because you took forever to answer your phone," she said.

"That's because I'm eating this delicious BBQ chicken dinner and my fingers are a little sticky."

"Sounds good."

"It really is," I replied. "I can bring you some. I ordered extra."

"That's so sweet of you. I'm hungry as a hostage. I was calling to see if you wanted to stop by tonight. My auntie and the boys left for New Jersey and won't be returning for a couple of days."

"So, what you saying Nikki?" I asked, licking my fingers.

"Boy, don't be difficult. You already know!" she said using my words.

"Give me a couple of hours and I'll call you when I'm en route to you."

"Okay!" she replied, hanging up.

I drove home and did about two hundred push-ups and took a nice long shower. After I called Nikki, I didn't know what she had in mind or what to expect, but this time, yeah this time, I was more than ready!

Three

A surreal experience happened to me one Saturday night when I was leaving the Watergate Social Club when, suddenly, a grey van pulled up beside me. Several masked men holding guns forced me into their van and handcuffed me. Right off the rip, I figured they were dirty cops until they began beating my ass! After several minutes of blunt-force trauma to my face and head, I passed out. That's the moment I felt, I was going to die, but as soon as the frigid ice-cold water hit me, I instantly woke up and my survival instincts kicked in.

Suddenly, I began swimming back towards the land. I looked up and observed the back lights to the van pulling away. All I could do at that moment was thank the universe for protecting me. Most of all, for Camp Young and Huntersville swimming pool, where we would practice swimming in survival situations like this often.

Was this shit real, or am I dreaming? It can't be because I'm freezing my balls off, but why would someone try to kill me? I just kept asking myself this same question over and over again as I walked towards the night traffic covered in a thick layer of mud looking like a zombie. I was still handcuffed from the front, my head was bleeding profusely from the gun butt, and I could barely see.

Luckily, the universe was working in my favor that night and I spotted my cousin sitting at the bus stop. He had to be just getting off from working his night shift at Hardee's. As weak as I was, I gathered enough strength to yell his name.

"Tony!? He stood up and looked in my direction. "It's me Brian, cuzzo!" He began walking towards my direction. It was pitch black, so he could only find me by following my voice, "Over here cuzzo!!!

"Bishop! What the fuck?" He began to panic.

"I'm okay. Call RJ and tell him to come and get us."

Tony dialed the number I gave him and my boy RJ was there in five minutes tops with three other homies and plenty of guns. They all hopped out and helped get me into his MPV.

"Bro! What the hell?"

"I'm good. Just get these cuffs off of me! "

We drove straight to Lowes Hardware store which was a couple minutes away. The homies went in to purchase the bolt cutters. They couldn't believe the story I'd just told them on the way there, "But who the hell would want to kill you?" RJ asked concerned.

I bust my brain thinking of who would want to do such a thing. All I knew was I felt blessed to be alive. Tony and RJ cut the cuffs off of me. After, I went straight home and showered. Then, I drove myself to the hospital where I waited several hours before being seen. Eventually, they called me, and I ended up leaving Sentara Halifax Regional Hospital around seven the next morning with thirty-three stitches in my head.

I was enraged and I felt betrayed. I didn't know who to trust anymore, so I vowed to myself, from that day forward, I wasn't playing any games in these streets. Ever since that day, I've never been the same cool laid-back Brian again. It was either Bishop or Big B. Trust me when I tell you, they were both with the shits and wanted all the smoke.

The year was 1998 and Jay-Z, DMX, Noreaga, and Ja'rule were taking the airwaves by storm. I'd just painted my Lexus midnight black and had my cousin Kenny Bug at Street Music hook me up with the top-of-the-line stereo system. Life was good and you couldn't tell me nothing. The more money I made, the faster I spent it. It was almost as if I couldn't spend it fast enough. Looking back, 1998 was a good year for me. I just wish I had invested my money better.

I pulled up at Nikki's house around ten-thirty that night. The lights were on, and I was happy to see that. She opened the door, and I was blown away by her beauty. She looked amazing! Her hair was cut in a Halle Berry-like style. She had on a leather mini skirt, Marc Jacobs stiletto heels I'd purchased, and a completely see-through blouse. I was turned on immediately. She leaned forward and kissed me. My god her lips were so soft and sweet, and she smelled amazing. I always love when a woman smells good, I thought to myself. I can't even explain the feeling. All I knew was, at that moment, your boy was bitten by the love bug.

She went into the kitchen and returned with a seafood platter. It consisted of a variety of fried food, such as coconut shrimp, crab legs, scallops, hushpuppies, and several types of dipping sauces. We sat and really got to know each other on a mental level. She told me how she was raised and the reason she lived with her aunt in the first place. I mean, Nikki had a testimony that would give you the goosebumps listening to. It's crazy because, from the outside, you would never think this young beautiful woman had been through so much. It took a lot of maturity and growth just for her to talk about it and I respected her for sharing.

We talked for hours, and I told her some of my most darkest secrets, trials, and tribulations. That night, we had a newfound respect for one another. It was bigger than any physical attraction because we had a mental connection. For that reason alone, I knew we were meant to cross paths. I ended up going to sleep around four-thirty that morning. We both crashed on the couch. Nikki got up around one and invited me to bed with her, but I knew what would have happened if I did. At that moment, I just wanted to soak in our conversation. I knew the sex would come sooner than later, so I wasn't tripping.

I'm an early riser, so I'd been up watching Sports Center for a couple of hours when she came walking downstairs. I glanced up and said, "Good morning baby. You look even sexier when you wake up. I know I have to marry you!"

She laughed and said, "I see you have that line rehearsed huh?"

"It's the truth," I said, looking into her beautiful eyes.

That's when she leaned forward and kissed me. We kissed for a few seconds, but it felt like minutes.

After, she asked me if she could be my girlfriend and I gladly accepted.

The more money I made, the more I began to stay away from Black. After I told him about the attempted murder on me, he began to get overprotective. Everywhere I went, he wanted me to check-in.

"Check-in? I'ma grown-ass man!"

I told him that I could handle myself. But I appreciate him checking up on me. I explained to him, that if It was a time I ever felt I needed him, I had his number.

RJ and I had our own trap house on 35th and Colley Ave. We averaged thousands of dollars per day. As usual, I would only stop by to pick up the bag, it was understood from day one that I didn't do trap houses and RJ was cool with it.

Nikki and I purchased a luxury condo out the beach. I even purchased her a BMW X5 that was fresh off the lot. She had been driving her Honda wagon for a minute. So, I gladly volunteered to upgrade it. I began driving and doing most of my runs in her Honda, because I didn't feel right trapping in a luxury vehicle. She would often drive it and come home telling me how females would follow her thinking she was me. She said she would roll down her window to curse them out. I would just laugh it off and say I didn't know who or what that was about. At times, I loved seeing her get jealous over me. It was flattering.

Our rent, bills, car notes, and insurance alone added up to fifty-four hundred a month, not including our daily fast food and gas. We both had AT&T high-ass phone plans, including shopping and getting my baby's hair and nails done weekly. So, hustling was all I knew. My standards of living had drastically increased, but for some reason, I loved getting to that bag. I had my own and money wasn't a factor. I just didn't have enough time in a day to spend it.

Two years into our relationship and me and Nikki were still going strong. Life was good. There were no complaints on my end. We would argue, maybe, once every three months. Nikki would often say that I didn't know how to come in the house at a reasonable hour. She would let me know she didn't appreciate it. She didn't care that I was the breadwinner and she would always threaten to leave me. At the end of the day, she couldn't walk in my house at four in the morning and still be my woman. So, I came home before midnight for a couple weeks, but you already know, I got back to it.

Now, there are a couple of places in Norfolk where you're guaranteed to bump into someone. One of them is the Feather n' Fin restaurant located on Princess Ann Rd. I met the plug there one Sunday evening after me and RJ left the smoke session at Miss Odessa's Spot. We called it the Bat Cave which was just a local hang-out where all the Uptown homies smoked weed and shot dice.

What's happening young hustlers?" we heard a smooth voice say.

I turned my attention to the older guy sitting by himself sporting a red Kangol bucket hat. "What's good ole' school?" I asked.

"The name's Ray," he replied.

I noticed he was a fly old head because his bracelet and Pinky ring had official diamonds. I figured he'd retired from the city. He looked like a merchant seaman or longshoreman. Plus, that SL550 Mercedes parked outside had his name all over it.

"I'm Bishop and this is my boy RJ," I replied.

"Well, I'm new to this part of town, but I'm looking to make some investments…if you dig my style," he said.

Dig his style? Me and RJ laughed. "Yeah, we can definitely dig it, ole' school," I said.

Ray turned out to be a blessing, he owned a restaurant called Mary's Café and two car lots. After getting to know Ray, I figured he was good peoples.

———————————

I came home one Sunday evening and noticed Nikki all dressed up and holding a bottle of champagne smiling from ear to ear. "What's the occasion, baby?" I asked.

She was ecstatic and couldn't wait to tell me. She said that she'd just been hired for the District Manager position at Cox Cable and would be starting Monday. Her starting pay rate was going to be twenty-five dollars an hour.

"Damn, that's good baby."

"I'm proud of you," I replied.

"Yeah, baby. I want to help pay bills around here too! You shouldn't have to foot the bills for everything," she said.

"But, I didn't mind at all baby," I replied while lighting up a joint.

"Well, I got the job already, so don't try to talk me out of it," she said as she stood with her hands on her hips.

I started laughing and I thought that was cute. At the end of the day, Nikki didn't have to work at all because she was my woman. I gave her thousands of dollars a month and I paid all of our bills. I knew I had to allow her to be great. So, I kissed and congratulated her on her new job journey. I went into our theater room and sat on my cozy lazy boy chair. I fired up the half of the joint I had left and began watching the First Take NFL highlights with Stephen A. Smith on Sport's Center.

While watching, me and Nikki's last conversation played over and over in my head until it began to manifest. When it did, I discovered a lot about my woman, whether she knew it or not. She understood that, in life, you have to have some form of independence and not be so dependent regardless of your current state or situation.

Also, it was her having the awareness that the income and lifestyle that I was providing for her had an expiration date and her being wise enough to know it could expire at any moment. This made me look at Nikki totally different after that day.

Four

The Berkeley reunion was everything they say it was cracked up to be. I mean, I saw everybody who was at, one time, somebody. Anybody who just wanted to be somebody was all there in attendance. Whatever car or SUV you could imagine was parked along the newly paved asphalt. So, what you drove didn't make much of a difference, especially if someone didn't see you pull up. Me and RJ saw people we hadn't seen in decades.

The atmosphere was a grand affair. There were hundreds of tents and vendors who were selling everything from food, clothing, incense, scented candles, and artwork. I estimated it to be well over two thousand people. The thugs, pimps, hoes, and hustlers all came out to enjoy the festivities. It was women everywhere scantily dressed in some of the most revealing and tightest booty shorts you could imagine. It was hard but I had to stay focused and remind myself that I was there for business, networking, and to potentially meet new suppliers and buyers.

My gear was lit, but I kept it simple. I had on orange, blue, and white mid-top, throwback Patrick

Ewing's, along with the throwback Mitchell & Ness Knicks Jersey. I also sported the plain Jane Rolex watch, pinky ring, and diamond bracelet for accessories. It was something light and not too flashy. I let RJ rock some jewels. He was dripped out with at least a hundred grand in platinum. We definitely looked the part! You didn't have to see what we were driving to know we were two official Uptown hustlers. We were in the building!

That's when I noticed a couple of guys that I knew who were from the Virginia Beach section of the city. They were all standing over by a large speaker conversing with a group of females. I recognized a few hustlers who I knew were getting to the bag. Me and RJ decided to push up because we were there on a mission. I approached the group of men with a relaxed demeanor along with a smile on my face. A smile on your face can change the whole outcome of any situation, especially when an unknown stranger walks up on a group of men.

We introduced ourselves and began networking throughout the evening. Within two hours or so, me and RJ had made connections with six to eight hustlers who were ready to purchase no less than half of a kilo. I noticed the nigga, D- nice, was standing in the background off in the distance. I wanted to holla at him, but he looked occupied. I made a mental note to

get with him as soon as the opportunity presented itself.
I was informed that he was one of the hustlers whose
product was floating around the seven cities, and I
wanted in.

Ray resided in Crystal Lakes. He lived in a
three-and-a-half million-dollar estate. He invited me
over for dinner and introduced me to his beautiful wife,
Sonja, and his daughter, Candice. Ray had cooks,
butlers, maids, and security. I only seen shit like this on
TV. His daughter, Candice, was sexy as hell and she
reminded me of the younger version of Lil' Kim. The
one-off of the Hard Core album. I knew she was a
freak the moment I laid eyes on her. Out of respect for
Ray and me getting to this bag, I dismissed the notion
of even entertaining that thought. Even though, it
seemed as if every time I looked up, Candice was
staring me dead in my face. I was happy as hell when
Ray finally excused us to his basement, which looked
like a luxury Best Buy.

We walked over to his mini bar, and he began
pouring liquor and taking shots of Hennessy while
listening to Teddy Pendergrass playing in the
background. Ray said what every old head says
whenever they're in the presence of a younger man.

"What you know about that Teddy P? Boy, this was way before your time. You were probably still living in nut sac city in '77 when this album was released," he yelled over the music in the background as if I wasn't sitting directly beside him. "They just don't make music like this no more, son," he said while pouring us both shots of Hennessy this time.

I never drink, but for some reason, I felt the need to. I wanted the energy between us to remain positive. I didn't want Ray to feel disrespected, so I figured a couple of shots won't hurt. It was time to celebrate and Old Man Ray was the plug. We took shot after shot, after shot, and before I knew it, I was as drunk as Cooley Brown from Uptown.

Ray knew I wasn't a drinker, he called me a lightweight several times and said I should have some hair on my chest by midnight. I laughed in return and explained to him that drinking really wasn't my lane. I knew he smoked weed too and I told him, I could possibly smoke him under the table.

He laughed and said, "You probably could, but the difference between me and you is, I will never do anything I can't handle. That's the moment you're most vulnerable and people take full advantage when the opportunity presents itself. Live niggas always stay on point, Bishop. I could have accepted you passing on the liquor. Cruise in your own lane and never switch up for nobody. Just something for you to think about."

That jewel stuck with me to this day. He changed the subject and went on and asked me what I thought about his daughter Candice.

"She is very pretty."

He looked at me and said, "But you never really looked at her the entire time we were at the dinner table."

"What difference does that make?" I replied, looking back up at Ray and laughing to ease the uncomfortable conversation.

He replied, "Most youngin' see a pretty girl, their mind get the racing, and they began to lose focus on the task at hand."

"My eyes were too busy seeing a pretty ass mansion with maids, butlers, and security detail. All I want to do is focus on getting to the bag. One day I will be able to call something like this home."

Ray started laughing, he looked back at me and said, "I knew I liked you for a reason."

He tossed back his fifth shot of Hennessy and fired up a blunt. Then, he looked at me and said, "Your lightweight ass drunk too son. I can't allow my

protégé to drive all the way back to Norfolk drunk.
Take the couch and sober up for an hour or two. The
remotes are on top of the television. I'll see you at
sunrise. We can discuss business over breakfast."

"That's what's up," I said. watching Ray walk up
the stairs and thinking in my head how Nikki was going
to have a fucking fit.

I got up and walked over to the bathroom and
the first thing I did was stick my finger down my throat.
I felt so much better getting the liquor off of my
stomach. I walked back to the couch to check my
phone, and as soon as I picked it up, it began vibrating.
I looked at it and noticed it was Nikki calling.

"Hello boo-tiiii-fuuuul," I said in a slurred tone.

"Why do you sound drunk?" she asked.

"Because I am!" I busted out laughing as if I'd
just heard the funniest joke.

"Bishop, where are you?" she asked in a
concerned tone. "You don't even drink. I'm coming to
get you."

"Babee, I'm waaaay in Portsmouth. I'll be home
in a couple of hours. I've been drinking and I have to
sober up before I get back on the road. Please don't be
mad at me!" All I heard was the dial tone. She hung
up in my ear.

47

Suddenly, when I put the phone down, it felt as if another presence was in the room. I could feel the hairs on the back of my neck tingling. I was definitely not alone in Ray's basement. Luckily, I didn't panic. I had that courage juice in me, so whoever it was, was likely to get an ass whipping like no other. That Hennessy had me thinking I was Debo.

Ray had this six-foot-long gold-framed mirror standing in the corner of the basement. I glanced over into it using the light from the TV and there she was standing in the doorway. Ray didn't know, but I had a photographic memory of that voluptuous shape of his daughter. Candice's lil' fine ass was stacked. "Why you standing there?" I blurted out. "Might as well come in," I said while sitting up.

She walked down the short staircase in her silk pajama booty shorts. Her hair was covered with a red-silk bonnet, and she was wearing the cutest Tweety Bird slippers.

"How did you know I was standing there?"

"I felt the energy shift in the room," I replied.

"Well damn! I hope it was a good shift!"

She had the cutest laugh. Candice walked over to the mini bar and poured herself a drink. She wanted me to see that she was half-naked…I could tell. I couldn't help but look the minute she turned her back. Ass was just all over the place. She walked over and sat down next to me.

"My father must really like you."

"Why you think that?"

"Because he never brings his workers to the estate."

"What makes you think, I'm his worker?"

"Because you are!" she replied while sipping her drink. "If not, you're about to be," she said boldly.

She took my Yankees fitted off of my head and began rubbing over my waves. "How old are you, Bishop?"

"I'm twenty-three," I lied.

"I thought you were like eighteen," she said.

I started laughing, "Damn, I really look that young?"

"Hell yeah! It don't matter. You're a man in my book or my dad wouldn't have never considered doing business with you."

"Is that right?"

"It's all the way right," she replied as she stood up and walked away. "Welcome to the family!" she managed to say before disappearing back into the confines of her father's beautiful estate.

Me and Black still kept in contact. I just never told him about Ray, my trap spot, or where I lived. I just didn't trust him, but the streets were talking. Finally, word had gotten back to him that I was doing my thing. So, of course, I had to put him on, but I told him that I had to go through my cousin Sean, and he went through his child's mother, best friend, and boyfriend who lived in Miami. Of course, I made it up. I wanted to make sure I distanced myself and the drugs as far away as possible from Black crazy ass.

On several occasions, I would cop a couple of bricks for him. At first, he wanted half a brick, then a whole brick, and then… Ayeee, out of the blue, this nigga, called me at two in the morning, talking about he wanted ten bricks. I knew he could afford them, but I also knew his MO. Black was on his bullshit. He would buy your drugs and kill you in the same day. It was no way possible I was ever going to allow him to fuck up this money train with Ray. I knew he was on his bullshit. So, I said what every hustler would have said to a hot-ass nigga at one time or another.

I told him that my peoples said that things had gotten dry and all they had left was a half of brick. I

know that wasn't what he wanted to hear. I could tell
by the look he gave me. I told him my peoples said that
as soon as shit get back regular, he would hit me up.
He shook his head and jumped into the passenger seat
of his black SL550 Mercedes Benz. A half of brick
wasn't shit to Black but a waste of his time and bullets.

I woke up the following Saturday morning and
rolled the fattest blunt of Kush. Nikki hit it a couple of
times, and we decided we were going to hit up Shoney's
breakfast buffet. Nikki was already dressed in red and
black Dior tights and stiletto red bottom heels. It didn't
matter what time or place, my baby was always on her
fly shit.

We arrived around ten and it wasn't even as
packed as I believed it would be on the weekend. Nikki
excused herself to use the restroom and for cautionary
reasons, I began scanning the restaurant. That's when
I recognized a familiar-looking man sitting in the far-
right corner. It suddenly hit me. I realized it was the
kid, Dee, from Bayside Arms that I'd been trying to get
with, but how do you approach a man of his stature? I
was on a mission, and I wanted my new plug, Ray, to
know I was the real deal. So, I boldly walked over and
said, "Pardon me, is your name Dee?"

He looked up at me with his hands firmly tucked
in his jacket and said, "Do I know you?"

I replied, "I'm not trying to intrude. I see you're out enjoying your morning with your peoples, but my name's Bishop. I don't personally know you, but we share mutual friends."

I began telling him that Ron-G from Bayside Arms was my peoples and at that very moment, I could tell he let his guard down and we shook hands.

"That's my boy!" he said smiling. We did two bids together at Lawrenceville and Nottoway. How is he doing? he asked.

That statement was the icebreaker. I told him he was doing what he did, getting to the bag, but to be honest, I hadn't talked to Cuzzo in years. I just knew his name was solid and well-respected in these streets.

"I just came over to give you my math if you ever wanted to buy some CDs and DVDs. I sell them single and wholesale."

"That's what's up. I love the lingo," he said while putting my number in his phone.

We dapped up and departed ways, but not before he said he would call me as soon as he left. See, a lot of people don't know, but it's no money like dope money. The place to be and sell it is out Virginia Beach. They tripled our numbers in Norfolk by a large margin. It was there, that Dee had always been known as that nigga!

I walked back over to my table and Nikki was eating while strolling through her phone. She never tripped whenever she seen me networking. She knew that came with the lifestyle and I loved her for that. Not too many women understood, but they wanted the benefits. Nikki was different.

We left and decided to go to Military Circle Mall. I needed a fresh pair of Timberlands and Nikki said she wanted a sexy pair of thigh-high boots. I constantly kept checking my phone to see if Dee had called. Just when I was about to say fuck it, my phone vibrated in my pocket. I answered, "Dee, what's good?"

"What's happening, Bishop," he replied as if we've known each other for years.

"Can you meet me Uptown at Big Daddy's in an hour? I asked.

"Of course," he replied.

Immediately, I called Ray.

"Hello," he answered.

"What's good old man?"

"Nothing much, youngin'."

"Enjoying life. You know how I do."

Ray was a slick-talking old head. Lately, I had been feeling some type of way. He'd been spoon-feeding me with the cocaine, but I figured if I could get Dee on board to score these kilos, then Ray would see that I could move bricks instead of this quarter key, four, and a half cocaine weight he'd been supplying. I told him I had a potential buyer and he was supposed to be meeting up with me later.

"What should I tell him the numbers are?" I asked.

"Just finesse your numbers youngin'. Always start off high, but end with a fair deal, so nobody feels as if they've been taken advantage of."

"So, do I front?" I asked.

"Not yet. That makes you look desperate to off your work. Good work always sells itself. Maybe the second time around," he replied. "By the way, my wife invited you over for Sunday dinner. If you can make it, it starts around seven."

"I'll definitely be there!" I said. *Anything to get closer to the connect,* I thought to myself.

Since I was in the area, I decided to head towards Ray's estate early. Uptown was infested with narcotics, undercovers, and the jumpouts were now driving around in luxury SUVs. I had other plans. I pulled into the driveway of the beautiful estate an hour early around six thirty.

This dude Ray was living. His front porch was all marble and he even had gold-plated door handles. I rang the doorbell, and to my surprise, Candice answered the door. *Damn,* I said to myself admiring this beautiful creation. Candice was looking better than she did the last time I was there. *Maybe it was the hair and makeup,* I thought.

"My mother and father went to Walmart. They should be back soon," she said, walking away from the open door.

I stepped inside looking up at the amazing cathedral ceilings with the golden chandeliers hanging high.

"My father called me earlier and told me he was expecting you. Come on in. You're letting all the cool air out," she said.

Candice was thick as hell. Automatically, I locked in on her backside. I mean, she was proportioned the exact way I love my women and she was gorgeous. Not to mention, she smelled amazing.

"Bishop!!" she yelled startling me out of my bae dream. "Is that your phone ringing in your coat pocket?" I looked down at it and noticed it was. "You better answer it before you get in trouble," she said laughing.

Candice even sounded different than the little innocent daddy's girl she portrayed around Ray.

"It's not what you think," I said.

I could tell she was feeling me, so being the bold risk-taker I was, I walked over and boldly palmed her ass to see how she would react. To my surprise, she turned around and began kissing me. I realized at that moment that she was also deeply attracted to me. It was about damn time because where had she been all my life. This new spark between us was just about to turn into a flaming wildfire. Suddenly, we heard Ray and his wife shutting their car doors. Candice tongue kissed me and cuffed my crouch before walking away and retreating back upstairs. She left me sitting in the living room with a hard on watching Sports Center. Minutes later, Ray and his wife walked in. I shook Ray's hand, greeted the Queen, and helped to bring in the groceries.

The following day I met back up with Dee at the trap house to discuss numbers. He went on to tell me that his connect had just recently received a life sentence back in New Jersey and that he was getting all of his cocaine from a third party. He was pretty sure he had been stepping on the product more than a few times before it got to him. He was starting to feel disrespected because he was paying top dollar, but getting low quality. He was pumping no less than six bricks of cocaine a week wholesale and three a week on the breakdown. *That's nine a week,* I thought to myself.

At one time, I honestly believed he was doing more than that. I began to ponder my next move, knowing it had to be my best move. So, I looked Dee in his eyes and said, "I can get them to you for twenty-eight flat."

To my surprise, he requested five bricks off the rip. That's the day our business relationship began and it was the first time I'd seen five bricks of cocaine in my life. Never had I seen or had the privilege to count that much money. Even though it all belonged to Ray, it still made me feel powerful. In just a matter of time, I knew I would be running my own empire. Ray always talked about leaving the game to be with his son. He would always say that he was nothing like him and that he was proud that his only son decided to take the legit path. He didn't sound proud the way he said it though.

Ray would always say I reminded him of a younger version of himself. That night, he sat me down and gave me some authentic street game. Two weeks later, I was shaking and moving weight like the big

dawg I was. Shortly after, I began to realize this nigga
Ray was paranoid as fuck! I had one hundred and
forty thousand dollars cash for him, but before I
delivered it, he wanted me to go through every bill to
make sure it wasn't any bugs or tracking devices
attached.

*Can you imagine counting all of that money and none of it
is yours?* I took pictures and tossed big stacks of money
in the air. I was amazed by all of those big-face
franklins. The more I counted, the more I wanted.
That's when I knew it was just a matter of time.

Eventually, me and Candice got tight. I came
clean and told her about Nikki and how long we've
been together. She looked at me and said, "You must
really love her a lot to still be with her."

I agreed, but one thing about men, we always
want more. We are hunters by nature and it's more of
the chase that turns us on than anything else. Hands
down, my girl Nikki was a dime and a beast in bed, but
I cheated on her every chance I got. Every time, I
regretted doing it because I would realize that it wasn't
even worth it.

Candice was different. She was a hustler and
she understood me. One sunny Saturday afternoon, we
decided to stop at Chick-fil-A in the mall to get a bite to
eat. That's when Candice revealed to me just who she

actually was. She said that she ran a team of hustlers getting money out in Elizabeth City NC. If I wanted to, I could drive down and set up shop at one of her five dope spots. Since I was buying my cocaine from her father, she didn't mind me selling it to her workers. I thought about it and told her I wouldn't mind taking her up on that offer. I needed a change of scenery the town was getting to out of control.

We left Chick-fil-A and walked over to Up Against The Wall, a more high-end fashion store. The minute we entered; we were bombarded by thirsty workers. They all knew Candice and how big of a shopper she was. The manager, Rick, and I talked for a few minutes. We just stood there and observed Candice looking and pointing as they grabbed. The melee of the three workers trying to be the best salesperson was a little chaotic.

I figured he thought I was her man, and he could convince me to shop as well, but I told him I was good. He went on to tell me how much of a valued customer Candice was, so I could see why they reacted the way they did. I watched as she graced the floor without a care in the world trying on clothing, belts, and even a sexy pair of Alexandre Birmam red leather thigh-high boots. The second I spotted them in her hand, I told her that I loved them. Her response to the workers was, "Give me three more pair since my boo like these." I was floored at her flamboyance and charisma. She reminded me, so much of myself.

Me and Nikki got into our first argument the following night.

"I can't take this shit anymore! You either going to do right by me or I'm leaving your ass Bishop!" she yelled. "I know my man. You haven't had sex with me in two weeks. That's not you," she said standing with her hands on her hips while wearing a silk bonnet on her head…still looking sexy as ever.

It took me by surprise too, I couldn't believe it myself. This woman, Candice, was draining me mentally and physically. I had to let up from spending so much time around her. I walked up on Nikki and hugged her. Then, I apologize for fucking up. She rolled her eyes and walked away.

Me and Dee became close friends. We talked "money talk" literally every day. We even decided to introduce our girls to one another. We decided to take our ladies to the Funny Bone comedy club one Saturday night. I can recall like it was yesterday. Katt Williams and Cedric the Entertainer were both headlining the show. We were all having the time of our lives, our women were getting along well, and the dinner we ordered was amazing. As the night began to wind down, Dee asked if he could speak to me outside. We excused ourselves and walked out towards the front of the building. Dee began looking around up and down like a secret agent. He even had me looking.

"Should I be aware of snipers or some shit my nigga?" I asked.

"Nah, it's a been a habit of mines ever since I was shot."

That's when he asked me if I could get my hands on fifteen bricks of cocaine. Immediately, I called Ray and he agreed to meet me at Captain George, an all-you-can-eat seafood buffet restaurant located in Virginia Beach just off of Laskin Rd. When I arrived, I drove around the parking lot until I spotted his white SL550. I parked a couple of spaces down and sprayed my weed-smelling polo shirt with cologne before I made my way in.

One thing about Ray was that he was always on time and he expected you to be as well. When I entered the restaurant, this thick ass chocolate woman approached me wearing a red shirt and some painted-on black jeans. She couldn't have been no more than twenty-five, she had a gorgeous smile, pretty light hazel eyes, and a nice ass. She walked up and asked me many was in my party.

"Did you say how much?" I replied as I started pulling out a stack of hundreds.

She smiled at my flirtatious advances, but I could tell she was with the shits. *Maybe another time,* I thought to myself. I was already in enough trouble with wifey. I pointed at Ray sitting at the bar and she allowed me access. I walked over and sat next to Ray.

"What's happening old man?"

"A whole lot of bills and the cost of living," Ray replied laughing.

He'd already ordered our beers, so I grabbed a plate and headed to the food bar. I loaded my plate with fried shrimp, coconut shrimp, scallops, clams, and snow crab legs. After, I headed back to join Ray at the table.

"So, time is money, and you are on the clock," he said looking at his presidential Rolex.

"You haven't even eaten your food yet talking about on the clock," I replied laughing.

Ray was just being old and terrible.

"Okay, you pay me ten thousand off every brick I sell, but what if I sell ten or even fifteen bricks?" I asked.

"All at one time?" he replied while tilting his glasses.

"Yes!"

"Not from me," Ray said. "It's only a set clientele that cop big like that. These little park boys' you're wheeling and dealing with ain't never seen two bricks of bacon. Sounds like a raw deal gone bad before it even happens if you were to ask me youngin," he replied.

"I disagree Ray. This dude, Dee, that I've been knowing for awhile…I know he's good for it." I said with confidence.

"I don't know. You're barely selling two bricks and now you want me to pull fifteen out of a rabbit's hat? That shit sounds suspect as hell."

"What the hell you mean suspect, Ray." I said because I felt offended. "I'm in it to fuckin' win it! I don't have time to be playing around. No risk, no fuckin reward. I see how you living and I want it. Just trust me my nigga! I can really make these deals happen, but if you decide to rock with me, I want a better deal."

"A better deal like what?" he asked.

"Like, if you allow the fifteen-brick sale, you throw me a brick and sixty grand. Then, we call it even."

"Let me sleep on it," he replied.

We shook hands and continued eating our delicious seafood platters. We never said another word about the drugs. We talked about how sexy and thick the hostess was, college football scores, and life in general. After we finished, we departed ways. I drove home, took a long hot shower, and watched a Netflix movie with Nikki for the remainder of the night.

<u>Five</u>

Me, Dee, and a few of my cousins decided we were all going to take a road trip down south to Myrtle Beach to relax and get away. Their annual bike weekend festival was taking place, and it was literally the place to be. I told Candice and she was on board. *So, much for a guy trip,* I thought, but Candice was trill. We rode together in her all-pink Range Rover. She was pulling two, top of the line, Ducati 900's. Of course, mine was yellow and black and hers was pink to match her truck.

Dee was driving his black Cadillac Escalade and pulling his Kawasaki Ninja 1000. My two cousins, Wing and Shawn, didn't ride bikes at that time. They drove a burgundy S550 sitting on twenty-inch Lorenzo's. By the time we arrived at Myrtle Beach, most of the hotels were booked. Candice, somehow, had the hookup. She made a few calls, and within a matter of minutes, we were all escorted to our rooms.

After we got settled in, I walked a couple of doors down to Dee's room. He was sitting on his bed counting money.

"Damn, ace! You brought the bag with you!" I said looking at the stacks of money piled up on his bed.

He looked up and said, "You never know when an opportunity will present itself. It's always better to have it and not need it, than to need it and not have it. So, I stay prepared."

"I feel you on that."

I told him that Ray was only paying me ten thousand a brick.

"Ten a brick is average," Dee replied. "He can do better, especially with the quality of work you pushing."

I agreed, but I knew that it was just a matter of time before Ray would begin kicking off. Plus, nobody from my hood had ever had a plug as heavy as mine.

We decided to grab a bite to eat, so we exited The Grand Atlantic Resort and decided to eat at the first restaurant we spotted.

"I'm hungry like them African kids," Dee said.

The first restaurant we walked up on was a damn Subway. I hate eating there, but everything always happens for a reason. We noticed two females sitting on a Bentley Continental smoking Black n' Milds.

"Now, that's what I'm talking about Dee," I said referring to their vehicle.

We entered the establishment and stood in line behind three females. One was light-skinned with long natural corn rolls. You could tell that the other two had tracks, but they were all decent-looking. The light-skinned one was the one. I could tell she ran shit. I could always spot a true hustler and leader.

Shorty was on her shit too! At first glance, I thought she was a pimp. Me and Dee pushed up and introduced ourselves. She said that her name was Missy and they were all from Baltimore, MD. She was actually there on business doing a little networking. Me and Dee looked at one another in agreeance. Then, we all took a seat near the back window so we could see everyone entering and leaving the restaurant.

Missy didn't waste a second. She said that she definitely had white Air Force Ones for the low. She was talking in code and referring to kilos of cocaine, but said that she would have to charge extra if she had to bring them to Virginia. She went on to say that her Air Force Ones, were top-of-the-line, fish scale designers and the least she could do was 15k. That was only if we were buying ten pairs or more, but she could DoorDash them to our front doorstep for 25k. She was looking forward to expanding her business with solid salesmen and future associates in different regions. We exchanged numbers and promised to call one another in a couple of days.

Missy left the restaurant before me and Dee, but on our way out, we noticed her driving away in that Bentley. Me and Dee walked away psyched up so much that we forgot to order our food. I hated subway anyway, so it didn't matter. I began thinking, *either Ray was going to play fair, or I was going to be teaming up with Dee and Missy on some other shit.*

By the time we got back, Nikki was gone. Her clothes, shoes, and the thousand belts and pocketbooks she had hanging up in our walk-in closet were all gone. To be honest, I was hurt, but I wasn't mad. I understood how she felt. For the first time, I respected her choice. I still believe, to this day, Candice had a lot to do with it. I tried to call Nikki, but it just kept going to the voicemail. By the following day, she had changed her number, but all I could think about was that we still had Missy's number. I called to see if we could score, but she was unavailable.

Dee still needed the fifteen bricks for somebody he knew in Chesapeake, and he was stalling them. If we waited on Missy, we could all benefit from that play. I called Ray to see if I could get them from him cheaper, just in case, but his phone kept going to voicemail as well. By mid-afternoon, Missy called back and we sealed the deal. We purchased fifteen bricks for

200k. Ray was charging 420k for the fifteen kilos, which was a two hundred- and twenty-thousand-dollar difference. That was a flip by itself.

Dee was just the middleman on this play, but that right there taught me a lot. The people you think are the man, are the middleman. So yeah, Dee's ass was actually in the same position as me. The bricks I sold were never mine either, but after getting with Missy, we both seen the vision. Pretty soon, we would be selling our own Air Force Ones with the profits made off of this sale. It was now our time to shine.

I was Uptown and hanging out at my old stomping grounds, Young's Park, one Friday evening. I was getting my car detailed when I received a call from Candice. Lately, I had been ducking her, because I needed some time to get my head right. Twenty minutes later, I noticed a four-door Porsche pulling up. I forgot she had my location on her phone. Candice stepped out looking like a million dollars.

"Why haven't you been answering your phone, Bishop?" she said agitated.

"I just been laying low, ya feel me? Trying to get my head back right."

"You want to talk about it? I'm here for you."

She could sense that I was kind of down because I would have normally grabbed her big ole booty and kissed on her neck. She went on to say that she had a surprise for me knowing how much I hated surprises.

"What is it?" I asked.

"First and foremost, I love you, Bishop," she said, rubbing my head.

"Why?" I asked.

"Because you always tell me that I'm beautiful, and that I'm better than the things I be saying and doing. You hate when I smoke cigarettes, and you always encourage me to invest my finances properly. You even took the time to show me how to start a business plan and how to get my LLC started. Most of all, you inspired me to go back to college…things my mother and father never cared to even talk about, as if we were just going to be Kingpins our entire life. Just like you were saying on our way to Myrtle Beach, 'Everyone and everything has an expiration date.' I thought being a dope dealer was the life until I met you. Why you think I'm so worrisome?" she laughed, looking me in the eyes. "I've grown to love you because you care. It's way bigger than this money shit with you bae, but I know you love Nikki, so I'm going to respect that and give you your space."

She got quiet, so that's when I revealed to her that me and Nikki had broken up weeks ago.

"So, what's the surprise?" I asked.

She held my hand and looked me directly in my face with those beautiful hazel eyes of hers and said, "Bishop, I'm pregnant."

Eventually, Ray thought about it, and decided to give it a go. He had his people bring the coke down from Philadelphia concealed in several hidden compartments in a Honda Accord. He called me around five-thirty, on a rainy ass day. Real hustlers love it when the weather is bad because we can make moves without worrying about the police.

"What's good Ray?!" I said, answering my phone.

"Aye youngster, I got that box of candy waiting for you at the candy shop. When can I be expecting you to pick it up?"

"Damn Ray, I took that play as no go since I hadn't heard back from you."

"Yeah, I thought about it," he said. "Figured I had a few days to sleep on it."

"Well, the buyer wasn't sleeping. He ended up doing business elsewhere. You know the game ace! First come, first serve. I was just playing the middle man, my gee!" I replied.

"I seriously hope you're not playing games with me, because I will personally kill you myself," he yelled through the phone.

"Damn, Ray! Where you get all of that animosity from? I've been nothing but a loyal true friend to you. You the one scared to make the moves that I'm creating."

"Listen here, ole Ray aint scared of shit. I've lasted this long because I'm cautious. Like I said, if you the police I'm going to fuckin' kill you!"

"I'm not going to keep taking these threat's like I'ma cold bitch or something," I said to Ray.

"I'll see you around," he said, hanging the phone up in my ear.

At that very moment, I was about to call Black and tell him, how much money, drugs, and guns there could possibly be in Ray's estate and storage. The thing is, Black never just robbed…he killed. Then, I thought about Candice and my child that she was carrying, and I brushed it off.

Meanwhile, me and Dee were headed to Baltimore to pick up the bricks. Missy said she would never come to Virginia, and she couldn't even see how we hustled there. Dee said some real shit to me on our way to Baltimore.

"Without you, this wouldn't be possible, so we can go half on these bricks, throw some cut on them, and up the annie. That way, we both come off with a nice piece of change."

I immediately interrupted him which cut him off completely.

"Listen Dee. I don't have a hundred grand just sitting around."

"That's okay," he replied. "Just give it back after we make a few flips."

"No doubt! Consider it done," I said.

Dee was like my older brother...we just clicked. Now don't get me wrong, I love my Uptown brothers for life, but I can't think of one of them that would have extended his hand to me the way Dee did. It's always an out-of-towner or someone from another city that will support or feed you. Your homeboys just want to be the ones shining and doing it big. Thanks to Dee, it was on and poppin' now!

———————————————————

I received a call from Candice around three in the morning. She was crying and I couldn't understand a word she was saying.

"Slow down baby, I can't understand anything you're saying," I spat into the phone.

"Tha…Tha…police just raided our house and took my Daddy away."

"Was it the Feds?" I asked.

"Yes," she replied.

"Where are you now?" I asked.

"I'm at my girlfriend's house sitting in my truck."

"Can you meet me at my condo in like twenty minutes?" I asked.

"Yes," she replied.

"And make sure you're not being followed."

"Okay," she said before hanging up the phone.

I couldn't believe what the hell I'd just heard. It all happened so fast. I began to think that Ray was going to believe I had something to do with it. Then suddenly, it was a knock at my door. It was Candice and she walked in crying. I embraced her and poured her a shot of her favorite tequila not thinking about my child that she was carrying. Immediately, I sparked a blunt because my nerves were shot. I didn't know what or if the Feds had something on me.

Candice went on to say, that her father had been on the run for over fifteen years. His brother and some of their affiliate's drug ring that ran from Philly to Miami had gotten raided and the word from the attorney was that Ray's name had just recently come up on a confidential informant's paperwork discussing grave details of his current operation.

"Niggas telling like some bitches," she said. "I'm happy you didn't get caught up messing with that Honda Accord because it was definitely being watched. They busted another buyer the same day while picking up the Honda."

She poured another shot and went on to say that she didn't know if the Feds knew anything about the money and drugs her father kept in the storage. They seized his boat and three of his luxury vehicles.

"Luckily, my mother's a doctor and could show her income because they were adamant about repossessing our house." She was so stressed she poured and took a third shot.

"So, you don't think it's any new charges he may have gotten arrested for?"

"No baby, I was there when the warrant was being read," she replied while pouring her fourth shot of liquor.

Those last couple of hours had been the most stressful times of my entire life. I needed to release some of this built-up stress. I decided to take a long hot shower. I excused myself and allowed Candice to get her thoughts together. This time, I noticed that she was drinking straight from out of the bottle while smoking on my blunt.

I entered the shower in deep thought. My mind was literally playing tricks on me! I had to think of my next move for precautionary reasons. I couldn't just go off of Candice's words alone. She loved me and she knew I would disappear if I had any inclination the Feds were down on me. Plus, she wanted me there every day with her throughout her pregnancy. I knew the count. I still had a plan though.

Suddenly, I felt a cold drift enter the bathroom. Seconds later, the glass shower door opened, and Candice was standing there naked.

"Can I join you?" she asked. Her eyes were bloodshot red, and her mascara was running black tears down her pretty face.

I helped guide her in and gently began to sprinkle the hot water on her until her body adjusted to

the temperature. At that moment, we just embraced
and allowed the water to trickle down our bodies. For
the next twenty minutes, we showered in complete
silence. Candace just knew what I needed all the time.
She even waited for me to grab the soap and bath cloth
before she took it away and began washing my body
while massaging my shoulders and back at the same
time. It felt amazing! In return, I did the same, but not
one word was spoken.

When we exited the shower, Candice went into
beast mode. I mean, I guess she can blame it on the
alcohol because I'd never had an experience like this
one. The sex was amazing!! This was one for the
books. I took notes and made sure for future reference
to always keep a bottle of Don Julio 1942 around.

We finally met up with a friend of Missy's. Her
name was Angela. She was a short and sexy redbone
with a stank attitude. Her overall demeanor stated that
she was just there to do a job and that was it. I
understood completely even though I was expecting to
do business with Missy. She followed us back to our
room. When we arrived, she stood by the door with
her arms crossed. Me and Dee were looking like to say,
where's the work? She looked at us like we were stupid
or something.

"Oh! So, apparently you two don't know how this works, huh?" she asked. "You pass me the money, I count it, and I make the call. When the drugs arrive, we make an even trade and we go our merry little way, "she said sarcastically. "This is the way Missy's does all of her business transactions," she said as she was sizing us up.

I could see the frustration on Dee's face, but that was Missy's hustle. At the end of the day, they had to play it safe as well. They were females who were shaking and moving major weight in a grimy, male-dominated drug business. Dee began stacking the stacks of money on the bed. That's when Angela pulled out what we initially thought was a duffle bag full of kilos of cocaine, but it was actually a money counter. After she finished counting, she made a phone call. Fve minutes later, three butch-looking females arrived with the package.

I could tell each of them had guns just by their hardcore demeanor and they were willing to shoot. I'm not even going to lie, I felt disrespected by this notion. *This wasn't how the exchange was supposed to go,* I thought to myself. I guess this is what happens when you have women playing checkers, in a man's chess game. Missy's pawns were out of pocket and exposing their queen.

We exchanged goods and we went our separate ways. Personally, I felt some type of way. I thought I was going to do business with Missy upfront. I wasn't feeling with that Charlie's Angels little stunt she pulled. Fuck it, we had what we came for. Now, it was time for me and Dee to get some rest. We had to be back up early to hit the road... I called my best friend RJ and asked if he could check on Nikki and the baby for me.

"Not a problem," he said before hanging up.

RJ was the only person I ever trusted around my girl. Bro has been solid since day one. You just don't find friendships like that anymore. The following morning, we were up at the crack of dawn, and we were out the door and back on the road. We decided we were going to make one stop only for gas and snacks. That's when I noticed a familiar-looking vehicle at the gas pump.

"Dee, isn't that the truck them dike bitches pulled up to our motel in?"

He squinted his eyes as if he was adjusting his vision and said, "Yeah, looks like it."

We sat for a minute and observed a pretty, short petite girl walking back towards it. The truck was unoccupied.

"Is she alone," Dee asked.

"Looks like it," I replied.

The female got into the SUV and drove away. Me and Dee looked at one another, and without another word, he took off behind her. We were on our bullshit. We decided to follow her, and she pulled into a residential neighborhood. She pulled up to a small condo. Dee parked three rows down, we grabbed our guns, and exited our vehicle quickly and quietly. We were down on her ass! By the time she put her key in the door, I held my gun to her head.

"You better not say one-word bitch!!" I said gritting my teeth together.

We forced our way in using her body as a shield until we realized that the residence was unoccupied. We literally ransacked the entire condo. The first lick we came across was the money we paid Angela for Missy. I heard Dee say he found the money under the bed in the master bedroom. Minutes later, he called me again to the kitchen and revealed to me two cabinets full of kilos of cocaine. Altogether our 200k and Missy's fifty-five bricks. Checkmate bitch!!!!

We gathered all of the drugs into a big garbage bag and headed for the door. I observed the young woman crying and refusing to look up at me. I asked her name?

"Crystal Johnson," she replied.

She said Missy was her big cousin and that she was just house-sitting for a couple of hours, but she still refused to look up at me as she spoke. She sat with her face in her lap shaking in fear. Dee walked over and whispered that she could identify us. She heard him and began pleading and promising that she wouldn't tell a soul, but at the end of the day, I knew she saw our faces too. I wasn't going to be walking around with that shit on my conscious. I told her, I wasn't going to kill her, but I was going to tie her up. She was okay with that. The silly girl even told me where the duct tape was located. After reassuring her she would live, I blindfolded and taped her hands behind her back. She sat quietly in Indian style. That's when I pulled my .38 revolver from the small of my back and I shot her in the back of her head. She never saw it coming. She didn't feel a thing because she died instantly.

I looked over at Dee and he was standing with his mouth wide the fuck open in total shock. I sent him to the car while I poured the gasoline I had retrieved from off of the deck near a weed eater. I proceeded to drench the entire living room. Then, I stood in the doorway, struck a match, and watched as the entire condo went up in a blaze of fire. We drove directly to the interstate. What was supposed to be a road trip to buy some product turned into one of the sweetest licks ever. Neither one of us spoke one word the entire drive back home to Virginia.

Could you believe how time flies? It had been over a year since I'd last seen Nikki. Me and RJ were leaving J-audio when we drove past the bus stop.

"Aye, that woman at the bus stop look just like your girl Nikki," he said.

I glanced to the right and caught a glimpse of her just before the light turned green. I bust a quick U-turn, pulled into the McDonald's parking lot, dashed across the busy intersection, and ran over to the bus stop. That's when I noticed it was actually her. She was so busy reading a hair magazine that she never noticed me coming. She looked even better than she did when she was with me. I guess I was stressing her the hell out.

"Hello, Nikki."

I was expecting a stale face, but in return, I received an enormous smile and a hug along with it. "Why are you at the bus stop?" I asked.

Since it was other's there sitting, she got up and we began walking down the street. She explained to me that she had met this guy and one night, he took her car while she was asleep and crashed it somewhere in Downtown Norfolk. She went on to say life hadn't been the same since me. She said trying to replace me hadn't been easy.

She let me know that she was staying with three roommates, and they were all sharing a two-bedroom house. She was currently attending Tidewater Community College and she was still doing hair for a side hustle. She had lost her job at Cox Cable due to transportation issues. I really felt bad for her. I hated seeing someone I love scrambling like eggs.

"But I see you still doing okay," she said.

"Always," I confidently replied. She couldn't help but notice the Presidential Rolex watch, diamond pinky ring, and bracelet glistening on my wrist. "Something light, but come on," I grabbed her hand and said, "You're going with me."

We crossed the busy intersection to my awaiting Mercedes Benz truck. I drove straight to my cousin Derrick's car lot, Luxury Autos, right off of Military Highway. We arrived and I told Nikki to look around and see if it was anything she liked. Then, I went inside to talk to Derrick. By the time we came out, Nikki was smiling from ear to ear sitting inside of an all-black ES300 Lexus.

"I like this one, Bishop," she said as she was touching and adjusting the switches and making sure everything was working.

"Cool," I replied. "Derrick is going to put a new inspection sticker in the window and throw a set of thirty-day tags on it for you."

I entered the vehicle and proceeded to pull out 5k in cash from out of my Gucci pouch. "The car is already paid for," I said. "This money is for your first month's rent and deposit for your apartment. Call me if you need anything else. I texted her my new number and I went my way.

I received a text later that night from Nikki asking if I could meet up with her at the Marriott in downtown Norfolk. I told her that I would. I arrived late, but Nikki wasn't tripping. She looked stunning dressed in her thigh-high leather stilettoes, tight jeans, and matching leather jacket. We held hands and walked a couple of blocks to the waterside and watched the moon set over the glistening water. We held hands and kissed the entire time. Needless to say, we had a night full of passionate sex.

Me and Nikki was back together, but with the understanding that I was also with Candace. Yeah, big dawg status. I guess when you pay like you weigh it's all good. I found out a month later that she was pregnant. I wasn't even tripping. It was about damn time because we had been trying for years to have a baby. I knew this wasn't going to set well with Candace because she was already nine weeks, and every day, she

wanted my undivided attention. She knew I loved
Nikki, so end of story. We can't take back what's
already done. At the end of the day, I was excited to
hear that we were expecting a second baby.

   *It's like, no matter how low you try and keep your
business to yourself, the streets will always expose you…good or
bad.* Word had gotten back to Black that I was running
with Dee from out the beach. Black's perception of
Dee being the plug was the same as mine until I got to
know him. I kept receiving blocked calls for two days
straight all-around midnight. I didn't think to answer,
but it just constantly continued ringing. I answered as
rude as I possibly could, "Yooo!?"

   "Bishop, this Black, adjust that volume down a
little bit for me homie. I heard you around town
slanging big work and that you partnered up with the
beach nigga Dee?" he said in an aggressive tone as if he
could intimidate me or something. *Little did he know,* I
thought to myself. "I know you got something lined up
for your boy," he said, referring to a lick or robbery.

   He said that he'd just took a major lost and
needed a quick come-up. It was at that moment, I
believe to this day, I jinxed myself. Even though I felt
like it was right thing to say at that moment, I told
Black that the Feds had just released me and that I was
out on federal bond. I also told him, I believed I was
being watched by the Feds and that's the reason, I

hadn't called or come around. I didn't want to bring any heat to the spot.

Immediately our conversation switched. Black sounded nervous as hell. He replied, "It's crazy out here in these streets. I got to run. Stay dangerous lil'homie. I'ma hit you on the back end."

I never heard from Black again after that day. When I did, I was at home watching the news when his face and name appeared on the television in big bold letters.

It read…

> **Montrell Morgan, guilty of capital murder, conspiracy to commit murder, robbery, mishandling of a corpse, and kidnapping, along with several class one felony gun charges.**

The streets would be a little more safer for the moment now that Black was gone.

Six

Things were going exceptionally well for me and Dee. We were finally starting to see some real paper and I needed it. I had a newborn and another baby on the way. My newborn's grandmother named her Tiffany Robinson. I was livid. The nerve of her and Candice. She didn't even give her my last name, but after a few months, Tiffany grew on me. Not saying I was cool with it, I just got used to it. I knew one thing for sure, I was going to be naming my next daughter Jada.

Me and Dee started to make so much money that we decided to relocate to Maryland, Delaware, and parts of the Eastern Shore. Norfolk was getting too gang-infested. Shootouts were becoming the norm and the Fentanyl crisis had the hood on fire with homicide and narcotic detectives. It was clearly impossible for me!!

Ray was in the Fed he was constantly calling my phone on some hot shit, so I changed my number. Candice told me she and her mother had recently driven up to Fort Dix Federal Detention Center to visit Ray. She said that their visit was going well until my name came up. He was throwing salt all over my name, He was saying that I couldn't be trusted and that I was a rat. He even lied and said that I was on his paperwork. This nigga Ray was on one. I guess a nigga will say anything when the odds are against him. Candace said she didn't believe him and she knew her father was being paranoid. She also knew I was as solid as they come. *Did Ray forget, I knew where he kept all of his drugs and money.* If old man Ray wanted smoke, I had no problem giving it to him. To this day, I still think Ray set me up. You just can't trust niggas.

One Saturday evening, he called the estate and asked Candice if she could go to his storage to pick up some money and drugs knowing good and well she was busy nursing our newborn baby. So, of course she asked me if I could do it. I told her hell yeah because I had plans on taking most of his shit the first opportunity that presented itself. His bitch ass wasn't going to be needing it for the next forty years anyways.

When I pulled into the Jackrabbit Storage Facility it was vacant. Not a car or person was in sight, but for some strange reason, I felt a bad vibe. I quickly brushed it off, because my plan was to be in and out in five minutes flat. Plus, my curiosity had gotten the best of me and I wanted to see just what was really in Ray's storage. As soon as I lifted the storage door, all hell broke out. All I heard was people yelling at the top of their lungs, "PUT YOUR FUCKIN' HANDS UP!!"

DEA agents were everywhere and were exiting out of the neighboring storage units with their guns pointed. They knew I was coming…this was a setup. I felt a bad vibe too!! I guess curiosity killed the cat. Thank God there weren't any guns or drugs left in Ray's storage. It was just bags and bags and bags of money. It was over three hundred and fifty thousand in cash and more in gold bars. I was handcuffed, detained, and transported downtown to the Federal Justice Center. There, I was fingerprinted, booked, debriefed, and charged with money laundering, and tax evasion.

Now, I know for sure that I had jinxed myself the day I had that conversation with Black about the Feds. I mean, I really spoke that shit into existence. Also, I believe Ray and Candace set me up. Luckily, five days later, I made federal bond and was released a few days before my daughter Jada was born. Me and Nikki were still holding strong, and so was me and Candice. I just didn't trust her as far as I could throw her, but the bar between the three of us was understood. My two baby mommas got along well. I guess you could say it was a family affair.

Life can be so unpredictable, I never in a million years would have thought I would be taking care of two households. After my federal stunt, I pump the brakes on hustling for a few months. I knew they had surveillance on me, so I walked light. Candace and I shared a condo off of 21st right across from the Virginia Beach boardwalk.

I put Nikki and Jada up in a newly developed condominium community in Chesapeake, VA. I was now responsible for two families, including myself. Money was going out rapidly, but nothing was coming in. I had six months left on probation and every day I left my house; I wondered if the Feds were watching or following me. I hated that feeling. I knew I had to get the hell out of Virginia soon.

I was finally at my breaking point. It was all or nothing. Dee had relocated and moved down to Baltimore, MD. He'd set up shop and vowed to himself to never return to VA, especially after my federal indictment. I called and told him that I was coming to Baltimore, and he was ecstatic. He said that everything there was going well, and he'd just scored ten pairs of the beige Air Force Ones. That's when I knew we were playing a different game. Now, instead of selling cocaine, Dee jumped head-first in the heroin game.

I asked him what made him decide to start selling heroin, and he responded that the demand was high for it in Baltimore, and it was no way he could allow all that money to get past him. He said that he'd made over a quarter million in a couple of months, and with the way his connect was throwing him bricks, we could be multimillionaires by the end of the year.

"That's what's up," I replied.

Since I met Dee, he's always been a team player. It was never the "just me" factor with him. It was always the "we factor." You just don't find those types of friends. Leaving Virginia wasn't an easy decision though because my babies were here. I wanted to be there and involved in their upbringing as much as possible. I loved watching Tiffany's first steps, and hearing her first words, "DaDa." I wanted to share that same experience with Nikki and Jada, but life don't work like that sometimes. We have to sometimes make choices that hurt us the most. *Nobody wins in this game.* I was once told that by my brothers a long time ago, and trust me, I took notes.

Fuck it! im going to ball out until I fall out, I thought to myself. I'm willing to live with my decision. I came into this game on my feet and I'll be damned if I leave on my knees. I looked at my Rolex watch and set my destination into my GPS. I needed some motivation, so I rolled a fat-ass blunt. Now, I was ready to hit the road. I called Dee back and told him that I'll be in Baltimore in five hours flat.

Baltimore was lit. Since me and Dee were the fly new faces of the town, the attention was all on us. Dee had a lot going on. To me, he seemed too comfortable in a foreign land. I mean, he had a group of young thugs hanging in the spot the minute I arrived. I wasn't feeling comfortable with the way he was running his, projected, million-dollar operation. It was already starting to look like a failed mission in the making. Some changes had to take place or I was going to pass on this opportunity with Dee.

To my surprise, he agreed. He said that he only kept the young hustlers around to motivate them to get some money. I laughed because I had to remember that Dee was from Virginia Beach, and they had the tendency to be green to certain things sometimes. To a Norfolk nigga like me, Dee would have been considered a meal ticket. Me being from Uptown, I'd experienced bullshit, fake shit, and larceny at an all-time high. I could smell a rat from a mile away. The only thing Dee was motivating was for them to eventually rob his green ass.

The four-unit apartment complex was perfect. I loved the setup. It had a main front door entrance that led to two apartments downstairs and the other two apartments were upstairs. Luckily for us, the people who lived in apartment #2 had moved days before I arrived. So, it was another vacant apartment directly across from Dee's apartment. I told Dee we had to get both apartments immediately. He agreed and had me go downstairs to tell Dana, a sexy dark-skinned chick, to call the apartment manager for him.

I mean, a good look at Dana had me hot and bothered. Not only was she gorgeous, but she was thicker than a Rally's banana milkshake on a hot day. How she got all that ass in them jeans to this day still amazes me. Plus, she had big titties and pretty feet. She called and was told that both units would be available in a week or two. That gave me enough time to map out this million-dollar operation.

Being from out of town, I decided to fall back and be observant. I sat on the front balcony for days on in and watched how the local hustlers moved. I clocked how many times the police drove through the neighborhood, and I watched whomever was watching me. It was no need to rush anything because I'd already had enough money to maintain. People soon began to notice me and started asking questions though. I introduced myself as Big B, a name I only used when I was on my bullshit. I told them that I was from New Jersey only because my BMW rental had those tags.

Eventually, I began kicking it with Dana. She had the sexiest laugh and accent. We were both high as giraffe thoughts watching Family Feud. After smoking our third blunt of kush, she told me that she was originally from Boston, Massachusetts, but had been living in Baltimore for the past three years. She graduated with honors from Morgan State and began her career as a paramedic here in Baltimore.

As our conversation deepened, I later found out that she loved hustlers. Knowing that, I felt like I could retrieve a lot of information from Dana. One thing about the drug game is that sixty percent of the time, it involves a female. A female can either bless or blow your entire operation. That's mainly because hustlers love to show off their cribs, cars, and money. Dana would soon prove that she was down for the cause. She told me that her brother and father were both doing federal life sentences and her mother died a couple of years after her father was sentenced.

She prostituted back in her college days to get by and maintain. She also admitted to having out-of-towners set up to get robbed. She told me that she and Dee had been talking for almost a year, but as far as she knew, they weren't in any type of committed relationship. She knew Dee fucked around on the regular, but so did she, so she wasn't tripping.

Now, all she wanted was a thoroughbred hustler who was about his business. She was willing to ride with him until the wheels fall off. I grabbed her by her hand and pulled her thick ass close to me. She looked me directly in my eyes and licked her lips before closing her eyes. That's when I knew she wanted me to kiss her. After our long passionate kiss, she led me into the bedroom. The minute we entered, it was on and poppin'.

I felt kind of bad because Dee really liked Dana. He talked my head off about her the day I arrived, but fuck it, I guess she liked me more. I felt as though I slipped up because I began telling Dana all my personal information like where I was really from, how old I really was, and I even told her my real name. Just the thought of me saying that to her made me feel uncomfortable. I couldn't believe I did that, but Dana seemed to be a solid female. I just didn't trust her knowing the real me.

Of course, once again, this nigga Dee was playing the middleman. Even with the ten kilos of heroin, he was only going to see twenty percent of the profits. I was livid because I felt misled, but what's done is done. I was already settled, and I knew I had to take the driver's seat if we had any chance of getting rich.

I called Candace and asked if she still had the trap house out in North Carolina. She said yes, but she'd already put someone in position since I decided to go to Baltimore. I couldn't trip, but before I hung up, I asked if she could front me a couple bricks of heroin to get back on my feet. To my surprise, she said, "Of course, why wouldn't I help my child's father? It's only one stipulation," she said.

"What's that?" I asked.

"You have to move back home with me, and only sell and distribute in North Carolina."

"Are you serious?" I was aggravated at her suggestion.

Candice was starting to sound like her bitch-ass father. I knew my woman like the back of my hand and this didn't even sound like her. I knew Ray was still in the driver's seat and she was just a pawn in this man's chest game. Ray was still trying to run shit from behind the wall. He wanted to keep tabs on his money and his drug supply. This time, it was clear he wanted to set me up for the kill.

So, like the gee I am, I told her to smear it on her back and I hung up in her fuckin' ear. The nerve of her disrespectful ass! Candace had me all the way fucked up. *What happened to getting money together,* I thought. This drug game was getting crazier and crazier by the day, but I was ready. Hell yeah, because I was crazy too and I was definitely ready for all the smoke.

Dee wasn't even tripping after I told him I'd smashed Dana. He shrugged his shoulders as if he didn't have a care in the world. Nonetheless, I had to tell him, and put him on game. I couldn't allow her to think she could finesse an official Uptown player! "No secrets amongst bros," was the motto. "Bros before hoes." Keeping everything solid. That's the only way, you can run a successful operation.

Dana put us onto a real Mexican plug named Victor Jesus. I remember the day we met him. It was just me and Dee. We pulled up to an all-you-can-eat Mexican restaurant to meet him. To my surprise, Victor was five foot three at the tallest. He sported a cowboy hat, some tight-ass Levi jeans, a pair of Italian leather cowboy boots, and one of the biggest gold belt buckles I'd ever seen. I knew he was the plug the minute I laid eyes on him. He offered us drinks and food. I respectfully declined the alcohol, but I accepted the food with lemon water.

For the next hour or so, we talked about everything but drugs. It almost felt as if it was a dinner date. I was highly confused. By the end of the dinner, Victor excused himself and asked me to meet him outside in the parking lot in five minutes. He said he would be sitting in a Silverado pickup truck. I exited the restaurant and walked over to his truck. Before I could get my hands on the door handle, I was ambushed by several cartel goons. I was patted down and searched for weapons before being pushed into the back seat of Victor's truck.

"Who sent you?" he asked.

"Dana told me about you," I replied.

"What did she say?" he asked.

I started thinking on my feet. "She just said it was a possibility that you may know someone who could help me find some good quality product."

He began to laugh as if to say, *you think you have all the sense.* "I like you," he replied laughing while lighting his cigar. "I may know of someone who can probably help you, but to fill your order and to keep it coming consistently, I'm going to need one million five hundred thousand in US currency by next week or it's no deal."

I looked him square in his face and like the big dawg I am, I said, "No problem."

It was at that moment when I knew it was all or nothing. I came in this game on my feet, and I'll be damned if I leave on my knees. I didn't know how I was going to get that money in a week. I just knew I would have it. Back at the apartment, me and Dee sat up for hours. Altogether, we counted six hundred and fifty thousand dollars. We had a week to make this flip, or it was going to be a no-go with Victor.

After talking to Dana, I learned that Victor was the top lieutenant for the Sinaloa cartel. Dana told me everyone she'd put on with Victor had gone on to be multimillionaires, including her father and brother. I wanted this connect bad. I had a week to get my ducks in order, and I didn't plan on eating or sleeping until I got that plug.

When I got back home in Virginia, I received a call from Dee saying he'd gotten robbed. I wasn't gone five hours and that bullshit happened. Dee said that the assailants kicked the door down and entered the apartment with both of their guns drawn.

"You said they?" I asked agitated.

"Yes," Dee replied. "It was two of them. The short one smacked me with the gun and began tying my hands behind my back. The other one ransacked the apartment."

"Did they hit the safe?" I asked knowing good and well the safe was in Dana's bedroom closet downstairs in her apartment.

"Bishop, they cleaned us out."

"But how the fuck they know where to look?" I asked.

"I'm just as confused as you, Bishop. Unless Dana rolled over on us!" Dee said.

He was trying to shift the blame off him when he was the one with thugs hanging all up in the spot. I was livid once again. Me and Dee were done! He had become high risk and a liability. There was no way I could continue this partnership. Before I hung up, I told Dee I wanted my bread, and I didn't care how he got it.

I popped up on Nikki. She and Jada were both home watching cartoons. Nikki was just as overjoyed to see me, as I was to see her. She told me that my best friend and brother, RJ, had been coming through regularly to check up on her and Jada from time to time. I appreciated my nigga for that. After she fed and put Jada to sleep, we went at it on the couch for a couple of hours. I watched her sleep while I sat up contemplating my next move.

Everything from that point seemed to be going downhill, because not only did our spot out in Baltimore get robbed, but Dana was also shot and killed outside of her apartment that same night. Things would continue to get worse. Candice called me around two o'clock in the morning hysterical and crying saying that her spot had also gotten raided in the middle of the night by two masked assailants. She said they shot one of her workers point blank range in his head and killing him instantly. They tied the other worker's hands behind his back and then proceeded to shoot him in the face and chest, but he was in critical condition fighting for his life. She said she felt as if it was an inside operation because they robbed her spot minutes after she received a fifty-kilo drop-off. I didn't want to say it, but she was better off fuckin' with me and Dee. To add fuel to the fire, a couple of days later, her father's Crystal Lakes estate was raided for the second time by the FBI and ATF.

The mystery still stands to this day, because Ray or Crystal never keep drugs at the estate, but on this particular day, their attic was loaded with kilos of cocaine. Candice was detained, booked, and charged with cocaine distribution, drug trafficking, and money laundering. I couldn't believe our house of cards was tumbling down. My back was now against the wall. I had a few days until I was to meet back up with Victor and I was determined to get this partnership with the cartel. It was all or nothing.

This had to be one of the best days of my life. Besides the bullshit I had been going through, I finally met up with the plug Victor. I paid him the hundred thousand dollars and just like he said he would, he fronted me one hundred and fifty bricks of raw heroin. With the right amount of cut, each kilo could possibly turn into two. It was straight to the top from here. I had my boy RJ back rolling with me too. He was my hitta and trained to shoot anything at any moment.

It was time to finally celebrate. We were about to be the richest niggas in our city, hands down. I decided to treat myself to a diamond Cuban baguette choker necklace and another Rolex watch for my collection. My next move was to hit the Mercedes Benz car lot. I already had the new Mercedes GLE 53. I walked into the dealership and told the dealer that I wanted the most expensive car on the showroom floor. It was time I started looking like the boss I was.

Candace continued calling my phone and threatening to turn me in if I didn't help her out. Just as I'd done to Ray, I blocked her ass. I had too much living to do. I didn't have the time or patience for the negativity.

Me and RJ would eventually become active members of the Sinaloa cartel. Money began coming in by the loads. I was easily estimating a million a week, easy. We invested in stocks, real estate, and purchased every mom-and-pop store we could find for sale. Dana wasn't lying when she said I would be a multi-millionaire with a solid year run. I was living in an eighteen thousand square foot estate on top of a hill in San Fernando Valley, California. I had another twenty thousand mega mansion in Arizona that was massive. I owned a ranch-style four-bedroom in Charlotte, North Carolina. I also owned an exclusive three-story luxury penthouse in Dallas, Texas. It was just up the street from the Dallas Cowboys football stadium. Throughout the year, I would Airbnb them out. I also had a twelve-car foreign collection. I owned two boats with a set of jet skis and two Ducati 1000 sport motorcycles. Yeah, I was rich as shit after I teamed up with Victor.

The cartel life was exceptionally good to me. I kept Nikki and Jada on the East Coast away from the chaos and the cartel. I had to protect my babies by all means. I loved and missed both of my daughters, but Jada was my heart. I'm so in love with that baby. I was there during Nikki's nine-month pregnancy. I even read her positive affirmations and purchased the entire Taylor's Magical World children's book series by Jae Davis for her while she was still in Nikki's belly. I wanted my baby to know all about the power of positivity and the universe. I also had the privilege to cut the umbilical cord and named her and Jada came out looking just like me. I had plans on marrying Nikki as soon as I got back home. I had finally made it to the top. I was just ready to kick back now and enjoy the fruits of my labor with the people I love and cherished the most.

I entered the Norfolk, United States Federal District Court on September 11th. I sat and watched by via video from an adjacent room. It was there I would be sat in front of a jury of my peers. I was scheduled to testify and give full details when asked about me and my co-conspirators for a fair plea agreement of immunity. Yeah, they had to play this game my way. I had the fuckin' leverage and I knew it. I wasn't going out like that.

Since a young adolescent, I've always figured out ways to get myself out of tangled webs. I rolled the dice big time on this one though. My life was literally on the line, but knowing me and my luck, I was looking forward to a clean sweep….456 Ceelo.

"The United States Federal District Court vs. Raymond Robinson."

"Good evening, Your Honor. The court would like to call our confidential informant to the stand. Do you swear to tell the truth the whole truth and nothing but the truth, so help you God?"

"I do," the C.I stated.

"Before the court proceedings began, do you recognize the defendant?"

"Yes."

"And what is his name?"

"I've always called him Ray."

"Let the court records state that the confidential informant identified Raymond Antonio Robinson, the defendant."

"And who is the defendant, Raymond Robinson, to you?" the DA asked.

"He was my connect," the C.I stated.

"When you say connect, you mean drug supplier?"

"Yes," the C.I replied.

"And what is the most amount of drugs you would say you received from the defendant?"

"Probably around a hundred bricks altogether."

"You mean bricks as in kilograms of cocaine?"

"Yes," stated the C.I.

"Thank you. The District rest its case, Your Honor."

"The United States Federal District Court vs. Michelle Lewis. The proceedings began with the follow-up. Do you swear to tell the truth the whole truth and nothing but the truth, so help you God?"

"I do," the C.I stated.

"Do you recognize the defendant and if so what is their name?"

"I do, but I only knew her by Missy,"

"How do you know Missy?" the DA asked.

"She was my connect."

"You mean drug supplier?"

"Yes," the C.I stated.

"And what is the estimated amount of drugs you think you purchase from Michelle Lewis?"

"I would say, around a hundred kilos, Your Honor."

"Let the record state that the confidential informant identified the defendant, Michelle Alexis Lewis. The district rests its case."

"The United States Federal District Court vs. Montrell Morgan. The proceedings will began with the follow-up. Do you swear to tell the truth the whole truth and nothing but the truth, so help you God?"

"I do," stated the C.I.

"Before the proceedings began, do you recognize the defendant?"

"Yes."

"What is the defendant's name?"

"Montrell Morgan, but he goes by Black, Your Honor."

"Let the record state that the confidential informant pointed out the defendant, Montrell Marquis Morgan."

"And who was Montrell Morgan aka Black to you?" the DA asked.

"He was another cocaine supplier."

"Have you ever seen him violent?"

"Yes. I've seen him shoot and torture individuals."

"Would you say he's a murderer and a menace to society?"

"Of course!"

"And how is your assumption correct?" the DA asked.

"Because me and Mr. Morgan have gone out of town on numerous occasions and have killed suppliers together."

"The District rest its case, Your Honor."

The United States Federal District Court vs. Candice Robinson. The Proceedings begin with the follow-up, do you swear to tell the truth the whole truth and nothing but the truth, so help you God?"

"I do," stated the C.I

"Do you recognize the defendant?"

"Yes."

"For the record, state the defendant's name."

"Candice Robinson."

"And what is Candice to you?"

"She was also one of my main cocaine suppliers. She took over her father's operation once her father, Ray, was arrested," stated the C.I

"Can you give the courts an estimate of the amount of drugs you may have purchased from Candice Robinson?"

"I've received so many kilograms...I couldn't tell you."

"Let the record state that the federal witness has pointed out Candace Monique Robinson as his drug supplier. Also, let the record state that Candice Monique Robinson is, in fact, the daughter of the notorious kingpin, Raymond Robinson. The District rests its case, Your Honor."

"The United States Federal District court vs. Deshawn Williams. The proceedings begin with the follow-up, do you swear to tell the truth the whole truth and nothing but the truth, so help you God?"

"I do," stated the C.I

"Do you recognize the defendant and if so, state his name."

"I only know him by Dee."

"Let the record state that our federal witness has pointed out DeShawn Williams aka Dee."

"And who was Dee to you?"

"He was another one of my suppliers."

"And how many kilograms would you say you've purchased from Dee?"

"A little over ten. He wasn't doing it as big as the others," the C.I stated.

"Was he also involved in the Baltimore murder of Crystal Johnson?" the DA asked.

"Yes, he helped me tie her up."

"Let the record state that the witness has pointed out DeShawn Andre Williams as one of his drug suppliers and co-conspirators. The district rests its case, Your Honor."

Two weeks later......

"The United States Federal District Court vs. Brian Bishop. You are charged with money laundering and interstate drug trafficking in the Virginia case docket # 1334520 of Raymond Robinson. You are hereby charged with armed robbery, arson, abduction, and capital murder in the Baltimore, MD case docket # 1245673 of Crystal Johnson. You are charged with armed robbery, home invasion, and aggravated malicious wounding of Travis Miller and two counts of capital murder of Wayne Rogers, and Corey Miller in the Elizabeth City, North Carolina case docket # 2345561. You are hereby charged with armed robbery, home invasion, and abduction in the Baltimore, MD case. docket # 0146533 of DeShawn Williams. You are hereby charged with the capital murder of Dana Smith in the Baltimore case docket # 3467800. Mr. Bishop, let the record state, you have openly admitted to each and every single case you have criminally been indicted for, correct?" the judge asked.

I pulled the microphone to my mouth and said, "Yes, your honor."

The courtroom's reaction went into an all-out frenzy. Family and friends of the victims shouted threats and were immediately escorted from out of the courthouse. This shit was playing out like a mob movie. I was making history. The prosecuting attorney said my name would be talk amongst elite serial killers, like Ted Bundy, Jeffrey Dahmer, and the beltway snipers John Allen Muhammad, and Lee Boyd Malvo. The difference between me and them was I was going home, and it was nothing they could do about it.

Then, this baldheaded prosecutor bitch, Keyshia Fleming, walked up. "Let the record state that Brian Bishop is a heartless, sociopath, narcissist, serial killer, and a menace to society. Let the record state that Brian Bishop also deserves to be put under the jail. Brian Bishop has turned federal evidence against his friends and allies in their underworld drug organization, in exchange for being granted full immunity. This isn't a win by far, yet, this is a spit in the face and a disgrace to our law-abiding, hardworking tax paying citizens. Unfortunately, another big letdown from our justice system. I rest my case," the district attorney said as she walked back to her seat.

Nikki sat while holding baby Jada with her mouth wide open. She couldn't believe what she had just witnessed firsthand. The man she fell deep in love with since a teenager was a stone-cold heartless killer. She felt trapped in a tangled web of lies and deceit. What was supposed to be a happy occasion, turned out to be a nightmare. This wasn't a happy day for anyone, especially for her and baby Jada. Bishop turned around and looked at her and smiled, It took every ounce in her gut, but she managed to smile brightly like a kid at a candy store. What else was she supposed to do?

"All rise! Mr. Bishop, due to your cooperation, you are hereby granted full immunity. You are free to go. Case dismissed!"

Bishop stood up and walked away with a devious smirk on his face.

Six months and fifty million dollars later…

I walked into one of Victor's exclusive mansions that he owned. I was patted down and ushered to the back of the estate by armed guards.

"My friend, Bishop!" I heard a voice yell from the Jacuzzi. Victor was smoking a cigar surrounded by several exotic-looking females. "Welcome to my humble abode. Care to join me?" he asked. The six beautiful women exited so we could continue our conversation. "How was the drive over?"

"Man, it was calm. Not too much traffic and the scenery driving up was amazingly beautiful. I seen a couple of estates I may interested in."

"Okay," Victor replied. "That would be your third or fourth estate? "

"My fifth."

"I can get my realtor on top of it. Just let me know and I can have everything set up for you."

"Cool!"

"So, let's get down to business," he said looking at Victor as he lit his cigar. "Bishop, I have a shipment of 800 kilos coming in Friday. I'm going to need them moved as fast as possible because I have another shipment coming right behind it. This one is a bigger shipment than your usual. Do you think handle this many in a week?"

"That's light, Victor. You know I can," I said with confidence.

"I have a spot out in Elizabeth City, North Carolina doing fifty to a hundred kilos a week wholesale. I have two more in Virginia, three in California, and five in Baltimore. They're all doing top numbers!"

"Okay, but before we move forward with the proceeding, I'm going need you to handle one more thing for me."

"Anything for you Victor."

"You see, I received some very disturbing news, from one of my FBI associates." Victor proceeded to open up his leather designer suitcase and he pulled out a paper manuscript of my federal indictment. "Looks like you ratted out everyone in your crew and was granted full immunity. That, my friend, is something I don't take lightly. I don't even care why you snitched. My question is, how do I know you won't or haven't already snitched on me?"

"Just believe me. I won't. I will never cross you, Victor."

"Good," he replied. "Then, you won't mind earning my respect?" Victor asked while lighting his cigar.

"It's whatever man. I'm just trying to get to this paper," I said reading my federal manuscript.

"Okay, in a couple of days, your loyalty for me will be tested. If you pass the test, you're going to be a wealthy man for the remainder of your life. If not, we can respectfully agree to depart ways," Victor said stepping out of his Jacuzzi, walking away, and disappearing into his massive estate. I got out after him and exited the estate.

I was driving my Porsche 911 down the Hollywood hills on my way to Los Angeles. I could only imagine what Victor wanted me to do. Whatever it is he knows, I'm with the shits. Nothing matters when it comes down to getting this money. I've made millions under Victor's watch. It was just no way, I wasn't going to pass his test.

Me, Nikki, and my baby Jada, were together in the diamond district in Washington DC. I went there to purchase wifey her own Rolex watch and a diamond ring to solidify our engagement. Nothing and nobody meant more to me than these two. Nikki was overwhelmed by the size of the diamond ring. I told her that was just the engagement one and she had to marry me to see the million-dollar ring. I had already purchased it and put it away in my safety deposit box. She kissed me several times and hugged the soul out of me. We set our wedding date for Valentine's Day in Las Vegas the following year. For the first time, I was excited to be able to make the love of my life and my child's mother happy.

Two weeks later, I met back up with Victor at another one of his exclusive estates out in Los Angeles. This time, it was to talk business.

"Bishop!" he said my name walking up holding a champagne bottle dressed in an all-white linen shirt and slacks sporting a pair of Ray-Ban Club Master sunshades, and smoking on his favorite Cuban cigar. "My shipment of 800 kilos has arrived. So, I'm going to need you to handle this assignment quick and fast… like in the next twenty-four hours."

"Okay, just lay it on me," I said.

"You made this hard on yourself my friend, but loyalty is what I stand on. You killed my friend Dana. She was Sinaloa familia. That was your first strike. Your second strike came with this federal paperwork. I normally don't allow anyone to cross me once and get away with it, but Bishop you're special. So, my friend, let's make a toast to the hundreds of millions of dollars we're going to be making together."

"Hell yeah!" I agreed.

We sat and ate some of the finest lobster tails, coconut shrimp, clams, and crab. I sat back and enjoyed the festivities throughout the night. That's when Victor walked over and said, "You have sixteen hours to complete your assignment."

"What you mean?" I asked.

"You have been here partying and bullshitting for the past eight hours. The minute you sat your black ass down, I said you had twenty-four hours."

"But you never told me what to do," I said looking confused.

I knew for sure I'd asked Victor to lay it on me. This Mexican was crazy as hell. Tired of whatever he was on, I asked for my assignment. That's when he pulled his glasses down to his nose and said, "In the next sixteen hours, your girlfriend, Nikki, and your daughter, Jada, are to be executed by you and you only."

I almost fainted hearing those words. My killer instinct kicked in, but I kept a poker face. Showing no emotion. I didn't want him to notice any weakness in me. I began looking around and counting the number of bodyguards Victor had walking around. I figured I could take Victor out, but it was too many armed guards. I figured I'd be dead within a matter of seconds.

Victor broke me out of my daydream. Then, he walked over towards me and said, "Sixteen hours Bishop. That's the only kind of loyalty I want around me," he said before walking away.

I stood up and walked out of his mansion drunk mentally. It was no way I was going to kill the two people who meant the world to me, but I knew if didn't complete the assignment, Victor was going to have me and them killed. That's just the way the Sinaloa cartel operated. So, I didn't have a choice. You see, that's the sacrifice you have to make when you dive deep into this demonic drug game. There's no morality, no peace love, or loyalty. None of that shit exists the moment you cross that threshold.

It is survival of the fittest. I didn't ask to be this way. It's just all I've ever known. I put money over everything!! To be honest, I'm fine with it. I can always find me another woman and have another baby, but it will never be another Bishop!

I entered our estate and observed Nikki and my beautiful baby girl laying on the couch asleep, with the TV on the Cartoon Network loud as fuck. I took the remote and turned the television down. Then, I kissed Jada on her little forehead and lightly smacked Nikki on her ass.

She woke and looked up. The first thing she asked me was what's wrong? Damn, I couldn't even hide this stress. It was written all over my face and she knew me too well.

"I'm straight," I replied. "Just some street shit bae. You know how that goes," I explained.

She sat up, began massaging my shoulders, and told me to relax. I told her that I loved her more than she could ever imagine. She said the same in return. I looked down at my watch. I had eight hours and thirteen minutes. This was the type of pressure I never experienced. Out of pure emotion, I jumped up and punched a hole in the wall.

Nikki sat there in shock, "Baby, oh my god what's wrong?"

Then, to make matters worse, my phone began receiving multiple texts. I ignored seven calls back-to-back until I decided to read them.

Nikki sat, holding our daughter, and looking confused and scared at the same time. After reading another one of Victor's texts, I tossed my phone across the living room floor in pure rage! I needed to relax, so I rolled a blunt, got undressed, and jumped into a hot shower. I stood in deep thought. I had already made up in my mind, that i was going to kill them, I just didn't know how. *Fuck it,* it was now or never.

Nikki's curiosity got the best of her. She needed to know just what the hell was stressing me out to the point of no return. I was too smooth and laid-back of a guy throughout our years together. She had witnessed me in some of the worst situations and I didn't act out this way. I was a thinker. This was uncharacteristic of me and she knew it.

Nikki walked over and retrieved my phone from under the kitchen table. The screen was cracked in several places. She began scrolling through my most recent text messages and she couldn't believe what she was reading.

It was a text from Victor. She knew he was the cartel boss whom I worked for. It read…

Victor: Is everything on schedule?

***Me: "Man, I'm on it. I'm just
getting home. I can assure you that
Nikki and my baby girl will both be
dead by sunrise.***

Nikki dropped the phone. She didn't know what to do! Now, she understood why I was acting so out of character. Her motherly instinct kicked in, and she hurried and took baby Jada next door to our neighbor. She made it back just in the nick of time.

She had already retrieved my Glock from the dresser drawer. She made sure it was locked and loaded. She knew the type of cold-hearted man I was, especially after my last court trial. I exited the shower and noticed Nikki was pointing my gun in my direction.

"The fuck you have going on that you have to kill me and your baby?" she yelled.

I stood emotionless. I looked as if all the life I had left was sucked completely out of me.

"I fucked up bae. I fuck up bad and the only way I can make this right with Victor is by killing you and Jada."

"That shit sounds ridiculous!" Nikki yelled. "We need to kill his ass," she replied.

"I wish it were that easy, but it's the truth. Now, I'm going to give you an option. Either you shoot and kill me now, or the first chance I get, I'm going to kill you. Then, I'm going to break Jada's little neck."

Nikki stood crying, "Bishop don't make do this bae!"

I began walking towards her with the coldest stare.

"Stay back or I will shoot you."

"Then shoot bitch!!" I launch towards her.

Boom!!!!

Nikki stood standing with the smoking gun in her hand shaking. She couldn't believe she'd actually pulled the trigger. I laid there with a hole in my chest while lying in a pool of my own blood and gasping for air. I took my final breath, looking down, as my soul ascended from my lifeless body. They say everything and everyone has an expiration date. Well, my time had finally expired.

Epilogue

"Order in the court!! Order in the court!! The jury has come to their verdict. Please stand."

"We the jury find the defendant, Nakia Suarez, not guilty in the premeditated murder of Brian Bishop."

Tears of joy flowed down Nikki's face. Her hell on earth was finally over. Now, she could move on and move past this tragic situation.

Two years later...

Nikki was driving down Virginia Beach Blvd. She and a couple of her girlfriends were celebrating her twenty-eighth birthday. They were all having the time of their lives when Nikki thought she'd spotted someone tailing her. Looking in her mirror, she quickly noticed that it was two or maybe three black cars tailing her every move.

With the quickness, she hurried and jumped onto the nearest interstate. Luckily, she was driving Bishop's Dodge Charger. It was fully stocked with a four fifty-four turbo engine under the hood. It went from zero to a hundred in six seconds flat…leaving whomever it was tailing her, lost in the wind.

Two weeks later…

An unexpected knock was at the door. Nikki was blasting the new hit song by Coi Leray while getting dressed. She glanced down at her Rolex to check the time. *Lemeka early as hell,* she thought to herself. She and a couple friends were about to attend the Sumthin' In The Water annual music festival located on the Virginia Beach ocean front. She had missed last years due to Bishop's back-and-forth federal trial, but she was determined to attend this one.

"Who the hell is it?!" she yelled at the top of her lungs while opening the door at the same time.

There, stood a Mexican wearing a white linen shirt, tight Jeans, a cowboy hat, and wearing sunglasses while smoking a sweet-smelling cigar. She glanced behind him only to notice several tinted-out black cars with armed security standing beside them.

"Hello, my friend."

"Hello, Victor," she replied.

"How you been?" he asked.

"I'm doing well," she replied.

"It's been two years and my legal sources have informed me that you won your self-defense claim against Bishop, just like I said you would. We had to set his death up strategically to keep the heat away from our Sinaloa familia. We set it up in a way that you would come out on top. Bishop was a dirty and foul individual with no morality or loyalty. I purposely pushed him to the limit to see just how far he would go. He had no ceiling when it came to getting money. He was indeed a selfish and dangerous individual willing to kill, steal, and destroy any and everything that got in his path. He deserved everything he received."

"I agree," Nikki replied. "Those texts on his phone made it an open-and-shut case for the jury. I'm just happy everything went as planned," she replied as she took a seat. "So, where do we go from here? Nikki asked.

"I have a shipment of a thousand kilos of Fentanyl, cocaine, and heroin arriving in one week. You think you can handle that?" Victor asked.

"That's light," she replied. "I have two spots out in Elizabeth City, North Carolina. They both doing a hundred kilos a week. I have the two here in Virginia doing the same, three in California, and the five spots I have out in Baltimore are all still rocking and rolling. We can basically dump off the entire heroin supply there and I can ship the Fentanyl to our West Coast buyers. The demand for it there has been higher than any other state."

"I see you've taken full advantage of Bishop's resources."

"Of course, one monkey never stopped the circus. The show must go on," she said laughing. "I'll definitely be ready for you when the shipment arrives. Thank you again, Victor," she said while escorting him to the door.

"See you soon, my friend," he said before disappearing into his all-black Mercedes motorcade.

RJ emerged from the back room holding baby Jada in his left arm. He hugged Nikki from the back while kissing her on her neck.

"So, that was the plug, Victor, huh?"

"Yes," she replied. "Everything's good now baby. The Sinaloa cartel is mi' familia," she said as she kissed him.

Well damn… the story of my life. You can't make this shit up. Like I said in the beginning, I inherited this lifestyle and the thought process that came along with it. Unfortunately, I picked up negative traits of the people who I looked up to and admired the most. I fell in love with the hustling before I could even count money, or even comprehend what to do with it. Loyalty and morality my ass! True hustlers know there's no honor amongst thieves.

Only the strong survive out here in these streets. The game is not fair, and no matter how much love you give, the streets will never love you back the same. It's eat or be eaten. I did what I did and that's that. Nikki will have her day too when she must sacrifice someone or something she loves to get to the top of the cartel ladder.

Good luck with that…What profits a man to gain the whole world and lose his soul? Well, I guess, I'll be having a meeting with the devil. All I know is, he better have his pitchfork ready, because I'm knocking at his front door with mine and I want in.